Big FAT Liar

Big FAT Liar

A novelization by

JOHN WHITMAN

Based on a motion picture screenplay by

DAN SCHNEIDER

story by

DAN SCHNEIDER AND BRIAN ROBBINS

A SKYLARK BOOK
New York ● Toronto ● London ● Sydney ● Auckland

RL: 5.3 AGES 8–12

BIG FAT LIAR
A Bantam Skylark Book / January 2002

ISBN: 0-553-48769-8

Visit us on the Web! www.randomhouse.com/kids

Educators and librarians, for a variety of teaching tools, visit us at
www.randomhouse.com/teachers

Published simultaneously in the United States and Canada

Bantam Skylark is an imprint of Random House Children's Books, a
division of Random House, Inc. SKYLARK BOOK and colophon and
BANTAM BOOKS and colophon are registered trademarks of Random
House, Inc. Bantam Books, 1540 Broadway, New York, New York
10036.

PRINTED IN THE UNITED STATES OF AMERICA

OPM   10   9   8   7   6   5   4   3   2   1

Big FAT Liar

prologue

My name is Jason Shepherd. At least, that's the name they gave me in the Witness Protection Program. You see, my dad's really a secret agent, and his cover was blown by some spies overseas, and we had to go into hiding, and so I'm not allowed to give you my real name, or you could all go to this really awful top-secret prison hidden under the Blue Ridge Mountains, where they just open a tunnel and pour in food once a year and leave all the prisoners to fend for themselves. . . .

Well, okay, none of that stuff is true . . . but then what'd you expect from a title like *Big Fat Liar*?

Anyway, my name really is Jason Shepherd. I'm fourteen and I live in Greenbury, Michigan, and this is what happened to me not too long ago. It may sound unbelievable, but hey, a lot of things I say sound unbelievable. But the funny thing about this one is that there's a moral at the end of the story. Another funny thing is that this story is absolutely true.

Honest.

I've pieced it all together by talking to the involved parties. So let me tell you a little story. . . .

1
one

I wish I could say the day started as out of the ordinary. I was sound asleep, dreaming that I'd mopped the floor with the best karate masters that Sony's PlayStation could create, when my alarm went off. I was sure it was a mistake—it felt like 4 A.M., so I figured my mom must have bumped the alarm button by mistake when she was cleaning the other day. I decided to ignore it.

My father's pounding on the door wasn't so easy to sleep through. I heard a *bang-bang,* and my dad's hurried voice calling, "Jason, you awake?"

I woke up with a jolt. The first thing I realized was that I wasn't lying in bed. I was on the floor. The second thing I realized was that something was stuck to my face. I swatted it away and the joystick to my Sony PlayStation went flying halfway across the room. On the TV screen on my dresser, two karate guys were frozen in midattack, with the word PAUSE written in big letters across the screen. I must have fallen asleep playing.

Bang-bang. "Jase?" my father's voice called through the door. "Up yet?"

I cleared my throat, hoping to sound like someone whose entire brain was in working order. "Uh, yeah, Dad. Been up for hours. Just getting dressed!"

Okay, so it wasn't exactly true. You'd better get used to that.

I was awake enough to know that it was a school day, and that I'd better put on some clothes. I pulled on a T-shirt and some pants, ran a brush through my hair so I wouldn't look like a total bed-head, and hurried out into the hallway.

My dad was standing there. His vital stats go something like this: mid-forties, hasn't lost too many hairs, hasn't gained too many pounds. I don't think he missed a single Little League game when I played. All in all, he's been a pretty good dad.

He had stopped in the hallway to fix his tie, and he flashed me a smile. "You finish that paper for English class?"

I nodded. And lied. "Did it last night."

My dad grinned. "Can't wait to read it, pal."

I hurried past him toward the stairs. It wasn't that I liked lying. Sometimes it just seemed like the best option.

I hopped up onto the wooden banister and slid down, timing my jump-off to avoid that little knob at the bottom that gets pretty painful if you miss your cue. I hit the ground running and turned into the kitchen. My sister, Janie, was sitting in the breakfast nook with one bare foot propped up on another chair. She was painting her toenails, a habit I find pretty obnoxious in a sister but which is pretty cool for all the girls at my school.

"Breakfast," she said, and poked her nail brush toward a bowl of steaming oatmeal on the opposite side of the table.

Oatmeal was out of the question for two reasons. One, I don't like oatmeal. And two, I didn't have the time. But if I didn't eat, I'd end up having a chat with Mom. My mom is very cool, but her "Breakfast is the most important meal of the day" speech is five minutes long, minimum, and I had zero minutes to spare. I looked around and spotted the solution to my problem. Our dog, Trooper, was curled up under the kitchen table. I grabbed the bowl and slid it down there. Trooper's tail started thumping and he gobbled it down.

My mom glided into the room from the other door and frowned. "Janie, please," she said, "don't do that at the table."

Janie rolled her eyes but screwed the lid on her nail polish, while I hurried past and waved a hand in front of her face that I hoped was good enough for "hello" and "goodbye." I stopped to give Mom a peck on the cheek.

"Jase, there's oatmeal. Did you get some?"

"Thanks, Mom," I said. "It was delicious. Got to go."

Out the door in ten minutes flat.

As far as I can tell, I have the best parents in the Western hemisphere. They support everything I try, they encourage me to do my best, and they work hard to set me on my feet when I slide a little in my grades or my social life. They even put up with my sister, which, as far as I'm concerned, earns them a United Nations humanitarian award. I might lie about oatmeal, but I'd never lie about my parents. They're really great.

They even got me the Razor scooter I was riding to school. I was just about the first kid on my block to get one. I had taught myself a couple of pretty good jumps, too, but I didn't have time for any extreme sports.

I was late for school and pumping as fast as I could when I saw a foot stick out from behind a hedge. My front wheel got jammed and the next thing I knew I was flying head over heels—not exactly the kind of extreme move I'd been planning. I hit the grass next to the sidewalk and sat up, rubbing a skinned elbow. When I looked up, I saw three guys looking down at me. They were about my age, but they looked older—especially the one standing right over me. His name was Bret Callaway, and he looked a lot like a picture of a caveman I'd seen in a science book, except that he didn't look as smart.

Bret was an all-star football player, an all-star baseball player, and an all-star pain. He usually picked on other kids, but I guess that was my lucky day.

"Nice Razor, Shepherd," Bret said.

I grunted and checked my elbow again. At least I could move my arm. "Bret," I said, "I would love to hang around and be physically and emotionally abused by you guys, but I should probably go to school."

I stood up and grabbed my scooter, but Bret punched me in the shoulder and I nearly fell again.

"Ow," I said lamely. "Okay, see, I had a feeling you were an excellent bully and I was right. Take it easy."

Bret smirked. "Give me the scooter."

I stopped. "You sure? 'Cause now you're going from harmless bully to hardened scooter-jacker. Are you sure you want to do that?"

Apparently, he was sure.

2
two

It was still ten blocks to Greenbury Middle School, and I had to run every single one of them. My backpack banged against my back and I was sweating, which I hate, but I made it to campus.

Just in time to see the double doors slam shut in the distance. They close the school doors at the last bell. The principal says it's for safety reasons, but I think they're just trying to catch the kids who get there a few seconds late. By the time I got to the door and looked through the smoked-glass window, the halls were empty. There were two signs on the door. One of them was an advertisement of some kind. It read: EXTRAS NEEDED FOR MAJOR HOLLYWOOD MOVIE—"WHITAKER AND FOWL."

The other one said: SCHOOL STARTS PROMPTLY AT 8:30. LATE ARRIVALS MUST GO TO THE PRINCIPAL'S OFFICE.

Which meant I was as good as caught unless I could come up with a brilliant plan in the next few minutes.

Kaylee sat in Ms. Caldwell's eighth-grade class with her back straight, her feet on the ground, and her hands folded on her desk. Everybody knew that was the best way to keep from attracting Ms. Caldwell's attention, and keeping out from under Ms. Caldwell's eye was the best way to get through English class.

Ms. Caldwell was born in the wrong century. She really should have lived a few hundred years ago as the evil ruler of a small country in Eastern Europe. Or she should have been the captain of a ship in the old days, when ship captains were tyrants. But since she'd been born in modern times, she had done the next best thing: She'd become an eighth-grade English teacher.

"Okay, people, no more horsing around!" Ms. Caldwell snapped. It didn't matter that the entire terrified class had already come to attention. Rumor had it that Caldwell had eaten a child once, and no one wanted to be dessert.

Someone made the slightest move to scratch their nose, and Caldwell growled, "Quiet! This isn't a rock-and-roll concert!"

Absolute stillness. Like statues. No one even blinked. A tiny smile cracked on Caldwell's face. She ran a finger through her hair to make sure the bun on top of her head was nice and tight. "Now then," she began, "I assume everyone has completed their creative writing assignments. . . ."

Kaylee looked like she'd tuned out the rest of the lecture. I knew she already had completed her paper, so she wouldn't be worried. I sent her a page. Trying not to attract too much attention, she reached down and popped her tiny Cybiko pager out of its holster. There was a message on the screen.

Look outside.

Kaylee glanced over at the window, where she saw . . .

You guessed it. Me.

Kaylee is my best friend, and she was my only chance at getting into class without another tardy mark on my record. The funny thing is, we don't have that much in common—she's a straight A, straightlaced straight arrow, and I'm, well, I'm unique. But one thing we do have in common is our preference for the latest message-sending pager, the Cybiko. Standing in the bushes outside the classroom window, I typed furiously.

Help! Create distraction!

Kaylee looked at me and shook her head. My heart skipped a beat and I threw her my very best panicked and desperate look, which wasn't hard to do because I was totally panicked and desperate.

Inside the classroom, Kaylee replied with a scowl, but then she slowly raised her hand. "Excuse me, Ms. Caldwell?"

Caldwell cast her icy glance at Kaylee. She would have bitten the head off of most students, but Kaylee was 4.0, and for that reason the teacher cut her some slack. "Yes, Kaylee?"

"Can you, um . . . ," Kaylee said, thinking fast. "Can you open the door? It's kind of toasty in here."

Caldwell looked like she was considering how Kaylee would taste with butter and salt, but she finally growled, "I suppose so."

The teacher turned toward the door. That was my cue. I grabbed the window and slid it open. Then I jumped inside, but I landed with all the grace of an elephant doing ballet and hit the ground with a thud. Fast as I could, I jumped to my feet. At the same time, Ms. Caldwell whipped her head around and I felt a chill go up my spine.

"Jason Shepherd! Did you just come in from that window?"

I turned around slowly, not wanting to make any sudden moves. They say rabid teachers attack if you make sudden moves. "What?" I said in disbelief. "No! You looked a little flushed. I was just creating a cross draft." To illustrate my point, I waved my arms to blow cool air into the room.

Caldwell didn't pounce, so I took that as a sign I'd stay alive for a few more minutes. I sat down and whispered, "Thanks," to Kaylee.

Ms. Caldwell returned to the front of the class, but her eyes hadn't left me, and she said, "Well, now that we're all comfortable, why don't you read us your story."

"Hmm," I said, thinking fast. "You know what, let's give someone else a chance."

Caldwell smiled the same smile I'd seen on a python once. "No, I think we'd all like to hear yours. You did do it, didn't you, Mr. Shepherd?"

"Ms. Caldwell," I said, schmoozing. "Can I call you Phyllis?"

"No."

"Understood. But the truth is . . . as much as I

wanted to write my paper, I couldn't. And it's because . . . because I spent last night in the Greenbury General emergency room."

"Is that right?" said Ms. Caldwell in a voice that clearly indicated she thought it was *not* right.

"See, my mom made Swedish meatballs for dinner. It's my dad's favorite, and he was so excited, he accidentally swallowed one whole. It was awful. He started choking. His face turned purple."

The class giggled. I kept going. "The meatball was literally bulging out of his neck." Now the class winced. "So we rushed him to the ER. The doctors worked on him all night. It wasn't until just a few hours ago that he managed to cough it up. I kept trying to write my paper in the waiting room, but it was too hard. I needed to be by my father's side."

I wiped a fake tear from my eye. "After all, he's the only dad I've got."

Ms. Caldwell nodded for a second. My story seemed to hang out there, kind of like a work of art being judged by a critic. Then the judge spoke. "You are lying through your teeth, you little demon."

Strike one. Undaunted, I kept it up. "I wish I were, Phyllis. Call my dad if you want. His number is 555-0756."

Caldwell raised one pencil-thin eyebrow. "I

14

believe I will." She whirled around and marched out toward a pay phone in the hallway.

The minute she was gone, Kaylee leaned over to me and whispered, "Are you crazy? You're totally going to get busted!"

"Maybe," I said. A second later, my cell phone rang, just as I'd known it would. I pulled it out of my pocket and handed it to Kaylee. "Say, 'Harry Shepherd's office.' "

Kaylee's eyes got huge. "No way! Don't drag me into this."

The phone rang again. "Come on, help me out! What am I supposed to do?"

Kaylee groaned. "How about write the paper! You have some serious procrastination issues, Jason. I think we should make a time to discuss this."

The phone was still ringing. "Okay, yes, good, let's do it. But that doesn't help me right now. Please!"

I stuck the phone up to her ear and pinched her nose to change her voice. Kaylee gave me a scowl that would have made Ms. Caldwell proud, then said into the phone, "Harry Shepherd's office. One moment, please."

She pushed the phone back at me. I coughed once, then said in the raspiest voice I could manage, "Hello? Oh, hello, Ms. Caldwell. Yes, it's true. I know I should've cut that meatball into smaller pieces. It was terrifying. I started to see the white light. I was ready to cross through to the other side when I heard the voice of an angel calling out from the darkness. And I opened my eyes and saw my Jason standing over me, and I said, 'Back off, Grim Reaper. I'm not done living yet.' And with every ounce of gas I had left, I burped that meatball right across the room. The doctors said it was a medical miracle. And I owe it all to my son."

In the seat next to mine, Kaylee looked like she was about to choke too. I ignored her. "I'm sorry," I coughed into the phone. "I should stop talking now. My throat's still very sore. Goodbye, Ms. Caldwell."

I snapped the phone shut. I love it when a plan comes together.

A second later Ms. Caldwell returned to the classroom. She gave me a look that was almost human. "Jason, I'm sorry. You just take your time handing in that assignment. Your first responsibility is to your family."

I tried to look forgiving. "Thank you, ma'am."

3
three

While I was doing my best acting job in English class, across town there was more acting going on. A Hollywood production company had chosen Greenbury, Michigan, as the site for a film called *Whitaker and Fowl.*

They were in their final days of shooting, and the two leading actors were sitting in a police car playing a scene while the cameras rolled and the lights glared all around them.

The actor sitting behind the wheel was a young African American man named Jaleel White. He wore a cop's uniform, but he also had on some very large, very awkward-looking red glasses. They were exactly the kind of glasses he wore as the character Urkel on a television show called *Family Matters* that had been on the air a few years ago.

As the cameras rolled, Jaleel turned to look at his partner and delivered his lines. "Listen, Whitaker. I'm not your brother, I'm not your girlfriend, and I'm not your priest. So if you want to stay my partner, I have two words for you, okay? *Shut the heck up.* You talk too much!"

The camera panned slowly to the other side of the car, and anyone watching finally got a glimpse of just who Jaleel was talking to.

It was a chicken.

The chicken was dressed in a little policeman's outfit and wore aviator goggles. The chicken let out a squawk and flapped its wings when Jaleel raised his voice. The actor blew a feather away from his nose and said, "Okay, can we cut? This isn't working for me at all."

A bell rang, someone yelled, "Stop rolling!" and suddenly there was a flurry of activity. The entire film crew, which had gone silent and motionless while the scene was on, suddenly went into action, resetting the scene, moving the cameras back to their original positions, and retouching makeup.

But no one went into a bigger frenzy than a red-faced man sitting behind the cameras. On the back of his chair were the words MARTY WOLF, WRITER/ PRODUCER, and that's exactly who he was. Now he jumped out of his chair and stalked toward the parked police car. "What do you think you're doing?" he shouted.

The film's director started to talk, but Wolf shut him up with a hand to his face. The producer reached the car just as Jaleel got out.

"Why'd you call 'cut'?" Marty Wolf demanded. "I didn't tell you to stop acting, Urkel!"

Jaleel fumed. "Wolf, I told you not to call me Urkel. My name is Jaleel White. Urkel was a character I played as a child. I don't even know why I agreed to wear the stupid glasses!"

Jaleel tore the nerdy glasses off his face and threw them to the ground. He started marching toward his trailer with Marty Wolf right at his side.

"Fine, *Jaleel*," Wolf said with a sneer. "Now what's the problem?"

Jaleel waved his hand back in the direction of the set. "I'm getting nothing from the chicken. I have no idea what my motivation is."

Wolf snorted. "You're a police officer named Fowl. Your new partner is a crime-fighting chicken named Whitaker. And your motivation is the nice fat paycheck that's keeping you out of working the drive-through window at McDonald's!"

Jaleel stopped short. "You'd better watch your step, Wolf."

Marty Wolf snickered. "No, you'd better watch *your* step, pal. You know how many A-list movie stars wanted to do *Whitaker and Fowl*? Several, okay? I put my butt on the line for you, but you keep screwing around!" Marty made a list of onetime celebrities on his fingers. "I'll get Kirk Cameron, Freddy Savage, Mac Culkin down here to fill your shoes so fast it'll make your head spin! Do I make myself clear, Jaleel?"

Before the actor could respond, a young woman appeared out of nowhere at Wolf's side. Her name was Monty. She was in her early twenties and she was exactly the opposite of Marty Wolf. She was cool, calm, and collected. I guess that's why she worked as his executive assistant.

"Marty, excuse me," she said in a gentle but firm voice.

"What!" Wolf barked.

"Sorry to interrupt," Monty said. "But Duncan's here. From the studio."

Wolf wrinkled his forehead, trying to dredge up a memory. "Which one's Duncan?"

Monty ticked off a list of facts. "Senior vice president of production. Wife, Shandra. One son, Atticus."

She pointed ever so slightly toward a man making his way through the set. Marty Wolf found himself looking at a very tall poker-faced African American man in a very classy designer suit.

Wolf walked right up to Duncan, grinning his biggest grin. "Duncan, my man! Welcome to Michigan. I'm flattered you came to see me."

Duncan looked about as happy as a kid in summer school with no air-conditioning. "Actually," he said, "I'm on my way to the new Keanu Reeves picture and the plane had to refuel somewhere."

"Right, right," said Wolf, unflustered. "It's all good. How's Shandra?"

"She's fine."

Wolf gave Duncan a little punch on the arm. "Oh, she's all that and a bag of chips. Your woman's like a parking ticket, bro, she's got 'fine' written all over her."

Duncan didn't change expression. Monty lowered her head in pure shame. Wolf didn't seem to care that his buddy-buddy act was falling flat.

"So how's little Abacus?" he asked.

Duncan's expression did change this time. It got more unpleasant. "Abacus is a Chinese calculator. My son's name is Atticus." Duncan shifted forward, leaning over the shorter producer. "Let me get to the point, Wolf. You're already half a million dollars over budget."

Wolf protested. "I'm dealing with a piece of

poultry, Duncan. It takes time to get a performance out of him."

Duncan continued. "Well, I'm dealing with the fact that you're in the middle of a three-picture deal. Your last movie tanked, your current one's not looking much better, and you haven't even shown us the script to your next movie, if there *is* a next movie." There was the definite feeling of a threat in his tone.

Wolf gulped but kept his face calm. "Do you know who I am?"

"I know who you *were*," Duncan replied pointedly.

"I'm Marty Wolf, okay?" Wolf said. "The Human Hit Factory. The youngest producer in Hollywood to have three consecutive hundred-million-dollar smashes."

Duncan didn't seem impressed. "This is coming directly from the president. You have one week to pitch us your next movie. And if it doesn't have dollar signs written all over it, you, the chicken movie, and your deal at the studio are over. Am I clear . . . *brother*?"

He must have been clear, because in Wolf's eye there was the faintest hint of a look of panic.

four

The bell rang, signaling the end of yet another glorious day at Greenbury Middle School. Before the bell had finished screeching, kids were already pouring out into the hallways and through the front door. Kaylee and I were two of them, but we got stopped short by a door that flew open. Out popped Ms. Caldwell, and that hungry look was back in her eyes.

"Ah, Jason Shepherd. Just who I was looking for. I need to see you. In here." She pointed into her classroom.

Kaylee gave me a look that said *Good luck* or maybe it was *I hope you survive,* and kept walking.

I turned into the room and instantly knew that I wasn't having any good luck and my chances of survival were pretty slim. Sitting by Ms. Caldwell's desk were my parents, looking very disappointed.

I was speechless, and believe me, that doesn't happen very often.

My dad stood up and shook his head. "How could you lie to us, Jase? You told me you wrote that paper."

I put my head down. I felt awful. The truth was, I usually felt awful when I lied, but I suddenly realized that getting caught was even worse. "I . . . I don't know," I said lamely.

Ms. Caldwell said in a crisp, mean voice, "Unfortunately, that essay counts for one-third of Jason's semester grade. Without it, he's going to fail the class."

"Which means what?" my mom asked.

Ms. Caldwell replied, "He'll have to repeat the course in summer school."

I gagged. "What! I can't go to summer school! It's full of weirdos and deviants."

Caldwell said, "And your point is . . . ?"

I gave my dad a look of sheer desperation. My dad knew what it meant. To a fourteen-year-old boy, summer school was like being sentenced to Siberia. No baseball. No vacations. No sitting around complaining that there was nothing to do. It was un-American.

As I think I mentioned, my dad is very cool. He turned to the teacher. "There must be something he can do to make this up."

Ms. Caldwell looked me over like I was a science experiment. Clearly, she wanted to appear sympathetic in front of my parents without letting me off the hook. This was probably all part of her plot to masquerade as a human being while her alien civilization took control of Earth. She said, "Well, I'm teaching English as a Second Language at the community college until six. If you get the paper to me by then, I'll think about counting it."

The idea of Ms. Caldwell teaching English as a Second Language was horrific. Since she didn't have any patience for students who already spoke English, I could only imagine how cruel she was to students who didn't. But I had bigger problems on my mind—like "A thousand-word story in three and a half hours?"

My dad nodded. "Should be no problem. Since making up stories is apparently your God-given talent. Let's go, sport."

So while I was trying to figure out how to make enough time to write a story, Marty Wolf was in his production trailer with a pretty young actress who'd been hired as an extra for *Whitaker and Fowl.* They were eating Chinese chicken salad together, and Wolf was wearing his most sincere expression.

"I'll tell you exactly what it is," he was saying. "It's the way you walked across the background of today's scene."

"Really?" the actress said. Her name was Libby (not that Wolf knew or even cared), and she had never been in a producer's trailer before. She had a feeling Wolf wasn't all that interested in her career.

"Really," Wolf said. "When I saw you do that, I said, that extra . . . that woman's got Julia Roberts, Sandy Bullock kind of talent."

The woman blushed. "Oh my god . . ."

There was a knock on the trailer door.

Wolf bit his lip in anger. Whoever had knocked was about to get fired. "I'm in a casting session!"

"This can't wait, sir!" Monty's voice came back, muffled through the closed door.

Wolf bit his lip even harder. Monty. He couldn't fire Monty. She was too valuable. He rushed over and jerked the door open. "Monty," he said in a very quiet but very angry voice, "what did I tell you? Unless someone died or there's a call from the president of the studio, you're never to bother me when I'm in a casting session. Now leave me alone and go rewrite tomorrow's scenes!"

He said that last part especially quietly. No one else knew exactly how much of the writing was actually done by Monty, and he wanted to keep it that way.

But Monty didn't leave. "Well, technically, uh, sir, there has been a death, so—"

"What are you talking about?"

Monty searched for words. "Someone . . . what's the best way to say this? Someone put . . . in the catering truck, and . . ."

"What happened?" Wolf bellowed in frustration.

"The caterer accidentally cooked Whitaker."

Marty Wolf choked. Then he looked back into his trailer, and his eyes fell on his plate full of half-eaten Chinese chicken salad.

5
five

When we got home from school, Dad gave me the Long Walk up the Stairs. The Long Walk up the Stairs came in two versions. One of them was the Arm Around the Shoulder. This one was reserved for times when I was sad, like when I struck out with a chance to win the city championship in Little League. The other was the Heavy Footsteps version, used when he was disappointed, like when my sister, Janie, first got pimples and I told the entire neighborhood that she had a contagious disease.

I got the Heavy Footsteps version up to my room this time.

"Look, Jase," my dad said. "Your mom and I love

you. And we always will. But if you want us to *trust* you, you have to earn it. You hear what I'm saying? No more lying."

You know, he could have yelled at me all the way home in the car. He could have grounded me for all of high school. But all he'd given me were the Heavy Footsteps clomping up the stairs and that short, simple speech. Now I looked at him. I looked him right in the eye. Usually when I did that, it was to show that I wasn't lying, even when I was. But this time I did it just to get a better idea of what he was saying. He was genuinely disappointed in me, and if you don't believe anything else, believe that that really broke my heart.

I wanted to promise not to let it happen again, but I was afraid I was going to start crying like a kid. So I just nodded.

"All right, pal," Dad said. "Now go in there and earn it."

I walked in and he closed the door behind me.

The funny part is, I don't think of myself as a liar. I mean, I know I've told some white lies, and maybe a few whoppers, but there's difference between someone who lies and a liar. Isn't there? When I was a kid, my mom always said kids weren't bad, they just did bad things sometimes. That's where I fit. At least, I hoped so.

I sat down at the desk in my room and popped open a bottle of Fruitopia, which is my favorite drink. It tastes fine, but what I really like is the cool green bottle. Then I pulled out a sheet of paper and a pen, wrote my name at the top, cracked my knuckles, and . . . nothing. I didn't have a single idea.

Something thumped the ground nearby and I looked under my desk to see our dog, Trooper, curled up down there. He kept his head on the floor but lifted his eyes enough to see me and wagged his tail some more.

"Hey, Trooper," I said, "you are so psyched you're a dog."

I scribbled in the corners of my notebook. I shifted my feet. I scratched my head. But still no ideas came. And the clock was ticking. Frustrated, I grabbed a Nerf ball off my desk and started throwing it against the wall. I had two bookshelves attached to the wall with a space between them. I called them bookshelves, but really they were more like stuffshelves, because I filled them mostly with old junk I had, like a model of Wolverine from the X-Men that I had put together, a boom box my parents had given me for my birthday, and an old baseball and mitt. There were also, believe it or not, a few books, but they were worn-out copies from when I was a kid—fairy tales and stuff like that.

Anyway, there was this space between the two shelves. When I was thinking, I liked to aim the Nerf ball right into that space. I usually hit four out of five. What made it even trickier was the poster of Shaquille O'Neal from the Los Angeles Lakers basketball team. The last thing I ever wanted to do was bean Shaquille O'Neal with a ball, so I was pretty careful not to hit the poster. It was a cool one, though. It was the one of O'Neal standing over the entire city of Los Angeles like he was a giant.

The nice thing about throwing a Nerf ball is that it really can't hurt anything, even if my throw is off and it hits one of the things on my stuffshelf.

But I didn't count on it hitting the shelf itself. Which is exactly what it did on throw number seven. The Nerf ball banged the shelf and (right according to plan) nothing broke. Then the shelf suddenly collapsed and everything spilled onto the floor in exactly the same way I figured Ms. Caldwell wanted to spill my guts.

With a groan, I went over to clean up the mess. It was going to take me precious minutes to do it, and I hadn't even thought of an idea for my paper. First I propped the shelf back up. Then I picked up one of the books that had fallen—an old copy of *Pinocchio.* I always liked that kid. Never knew why. As I put it back on the shelf, my eyes traveled from the picture of Pinocchio to the big poster of Shaquille O'Neal towering over the city. Then Pinocchio again, with his nose growing even longer after telling a lie. Then Shaq. Then my green Fruitopia bottle. Then Pinocchio.

Then I got the idea.

I don't know how it came. I don't know why. All I know is that for the next two hours I was a human word processor. It was like the words were flowing out of the end of my pen and I was just trying to keep up. My dad had been joking, but maybe he was right. Maybe telling stories was my talent. I'd never really had one before. I mean, I do okay in school, but I've never been one of those people you look at and say, "Oh, yeah, Jason, he's the best this at school, or the best that in the neighborhood." But now, for those two hours, sitting at that desk, I was the best at something. I was telling a story, and it was good. Time went by in a blink. When I was done, I was gasping for breath like I'd just finished a sprint. I think I was actually sweating. But it was done. I had my story. On the cover, in huge letters, I wrote the title.

BIG FAT LIAR.

I glanced at the clock: 4:45. That didn't give me a whole lot of time.

Grabbing my notebook, I dashed out of the room and down the stairs.

The Long Walk up the Stairs was replaced by the Insane Run down at Breakneck Speed. I think I only touched one or two steps before I hit bottom and hung a hard right to the garage door. It was only when I reached the garage that I realized I had a real problem on my hands.

Bret Callaway. "Why'd he have to steal the scooter today!" I said.

There was only one other mode of transportation in the garage, and I didn't like it. But I didn't have a choice.

SIX

Five minutes later I was pedaling down my street on a pink bicycle with a banana seat (with built-in glitter), butterfly stickers, streamers on the handlebars, and a little license plate that read JANIE.

Man, I wish I actually was lying about that part.

But there I was, tooling through my neighborhood on the girliest of all girl bikes. My only hope was to ride as fast as I could so that fewer people would have the chance to see me. I kept saying in my head, *Oh, please, please, don't let anyone see me. I'll do anything, I'll be a great kid, I'll never tell another lie just so long as no one—*

"Shepherd!"

Murphy's Law says that anything that can go wrong will go wrong. Well, Murphy must have lived in my neighborhood, because no sooner had I made my wish than Bret Callaway and his two ultrajock clones rounded the corner, football gear in hand.

"Nice bike, Shepherd!" Bret roared. "You going to buy yourself a new dress?"

"Yeah," I said. "Yours doesn't fit me anymore!"

Not a bad comeback, I thought. Maybe a little bit like sixth grade, but better than nothing.

I pedaled faster, rounding a corner before Bret's slow-as-molasses brain could think of a reply. I took the corner a little fast and scooted off the sidewalk and into the street before I noticed something big, black, and hurtling right at me. The accident happened so fast my life didn't even have time to flash before my eyes. Suddenly the bike flew out from under me, I did a somersault over the hood of a car, and then I was sitting in the middle of the street. Somewhere, way off, I heard tires squealing; then a door opened and closed and I heard footsteps. Someone touched my shoulder and I looked up.

There was a man standing over me dressed in a black suit with a black cap. "You all right there, buddy? You hurt?"

I didn't think I was hurt. I just didn't know how

I'd been riding a bicycle one minute and sitting in the street the next. "Um, yeah. I guess."

The man helped me up and I realized I was standing next to a limousine. It had stopped a few feet from me. Underneath the front of the big black car I could see a mess of pink metal, squished butterflies, and crumpled streamers. My sister's bicycle.

The limousine driver whistled. "That could've been you."

I said, "If I was that bike, I'd *want* to be hit by a car."

The back door of the limousine opened and Marty Wolf stepped out. Of course I didn't know it was Marty Wolf then. He was just a guy with a big mouth and an ear glued to a cell phone. He was shouting into it. "I don't care if he's about to get slaughtered. Pull him out of the line, stick him in a freakin' Fed Ex package, and ship him down here. I need a chicken that can act!"

"Sir," the limo driver said.

"Wait," Wolf said.

"But, sir—"

"I'm on the phone!"

"I think we just hit this kid."

Wolf looked at the car and the twisted pink bike. "Is the limo all right?"

The driver looked at me again. He seemed genuinely concerned. "You sure you're all right?"

I suddenly remembered why I'd been in a hurry. "Yeah, yeah, but you've got to help me out. I need to get to the community college in two minutes or else I'm going to fail eighth grade."

Wolf clicked off his phone and checked his watch. "What's the holdup here?"

The limo driver explained. "The kid says he needs a ride to the community college."

Wolf snorted. "What am I running, a taxi service?"

The driver frowned. "We did almost run him over."

Wolf held up his hands with a look of innocence. "No, *you* almost ran him over. I was just the passenger."

"Come on, it's right down the road. You're lucky I don't sue you for whiplash." That gave me an idea, of course, and I immediately started to rub my neck. "Actually, my neck does feel pretty stiff."

Wolf snorted again. "Get in the car."

I climbed into the wide-open passenger area of the stretch limo. There were couches facing forward and back, a television, and a minibar. I sat and plopped my backpack down. "Oh, man, if you knew what kind of day I had . . ."

Wolf sat across from me. "Yeah, well, I bet your star actor didn't get eaten."

"Well," I said, "no. But it's been a bad day anyway."

The minibar looked good. I glanced at Wolf, who nodded, and I reached over for a Coke. As I did, my backpack spilled onto the floor, notebooks and all. I grabbed them all up and stuffed them back in, but I didn't see everything. Man, I wish I'd seen everything!

"It must be tough to be eleven," said Wolf, who didn't seem to have much sympathy for anyone else.

"Actually, I'm fourteen," I said.

"My mistake," said Wolf.

This guy didn't seem like he was going to win any good citizenship awards, but he was giving me the ride that might save my life, so I held out my hand and said, "Jason Shepherd."

He took it, shook it once, and said, "Marty Wolf." He had a good handshake. My father always told me you should pay attention to a person's handshake.

I sat back against the couch. "Nice wheels," I said, trying to sound like someone who'd been in several hundred limos. "Nice couch, too. What is it, leather?"

Wolf nodded. "Corinthian."

"The finest," I said, wondering what the heck a Corinthian was. "Made from llama skin, right?"

"Wild boar," Wolf said, as if everyone knew that

Corinthian leather was made from wild boar. I looked at his face. It was deadpan, flat, totally honest. But heck, I'm a pro.

"You're lying to me, right?" I said.

"Yes, I am," Wolf said with that same deadpan face.

"Why?"

Now Marty Wolf yawned. "Because the truth's overrated, kid."

"Now, see!" I said. "That's what I keep telling people. Only it sure as heck doesn't get me a limo."

Wolf checked his watch. "Well, you're in this one, aren't you?"

The limo driver's voice came over a little speaker hidden somewhere in the back. "Community college." I felt the car slow down. I opened the door and jumped out. "Thanks for the ride, gentlemen."

I slammed the door and ran toward the small collection of community college buildings. I never looked back. I don't know if Marty Wolf ever tried to get my attention. He hasn't been very willing to talk to me since all this happened.

As the limo rolled forward, Wolf must have noticed a little notebook on the floor. He must have picked it up and started reading the opening paragraphs of *Big Fat Liar*. And then he must have started to smile.

7
seven

"**I left** it in the limo."

I was standing in the dingy community college classroom where Ms. Caldwell taught her English as a Second Language class. My parents were there too—Ms. Caldwell had called them twenty minutes earlier, after I'd told her my story. She and I hadn't said a word since then. The minute I'd started looking for my notebook and realized it was gone, she'd held up her hand and dialed a phone—her own cell phone this time—and called my parents. Now they were sitting across from me under the yellow-green fluorescent bulbs.

"I left it in the limo," I said again.

My mom rolled her eyes. "Oh, good God . . ."

"I swear!" I nearly yelled. "The story was in my backpack when I left the house. I was riding down the street on Janie's old Schwinn and some limo hit me. They offered me a ride and I accidentally spilled all my stuff when I got in. I must've forgotten to take the paper."

My mom said sternly, "Give us one good reason why we should believe you."

"Because it's true! There was a guy in the back of the limo. Marty something. Maybe he took it."

Ms. Caldwell licked her lips. "Of course he did. There's quite a big black market for eighth-grade English papers. He's probably selling it on eBay as we speak."

I looked at my father. "Dad, I'm telling the truth. You've got to believe me."

I had a weird feeling in the pit of my stomach. I felt like one of those guys in an old episode of *The Twilight Zone*, where he's the same but everyone around him has suddenly changed into something else, only they don't know it. I was speaking facts, but they didn't understand them.

My father fidgeted. "I want to believe you, Jase, but you make that just about impossible."

Impossible to believe me. What was I supposed

to do—make up a story? Should I lie and tell them something they'd believe? I was totally bewildered.

My mother turned to Ms. Caldwell. "What are our options?"

A thin, wicked smile crossed Ms. Caldwell's lips. "Summer school."

eight

Let's fast-forward to the end of the school year. Okay, so imagine that you have to wear wool underwear that's a size too small for you, and socks made out of sandpaper. And shoes that have tacks poking through the bottom, along with a jacket that's too short and pinches under your armpits and a shirt with a collar you have to button up. And a bow tie. Imagine that.

It would be heaven compared to summer school.

The worst part of summer school—worse than the heat, worse than the boring teachers—is the feeling of failure. Everyone in the classroom has failed at something. The depression fills the room with a stink worse than Bret Callaway's armpits.

The kids who were forced to be there had failed at something, and the kids who had chosen to be there . . . well, they were just losers. I mean, even the bookworms and the brains were off at camp somewhere building rockets or learning to become librarians or something.

"You must have made at least one friend," Kaylee said. It was Thursday afternoon two weeks into summer school. Kaylee knew how miserable I was, and since summer classes ended at one o'clock, she'd offered to take me to a movie. We were going to Googleplex, which had about a jillion screens.

As we walked into the theater, I said, "A friend? Oh, yeah, the kid behind me who keeps flicking his boogers at the back of my head seems like a nice guy." We handed our tickets over and walked across the lobby. "I shouldn't even be in summer school."

"If it makes you feel any better," Kaylee said as we turned the corner to our screen, "my parents decided they needed an adventure, so they're taking a river-rafting trip in the Grand Canyon."

"You're going camping at one of the natural wonders of the world, and I'm dodging boogers," I said snippily. "Yeah. I feel so much better. Thanks."

"*They're* going," Kaylee corrected. "My big adventure is staying over at my grandma Pearl's with her toe fungus."

I grimaced. I'd met Grandma Pearl. Kaylee wasn't kidding about the fungus. "Well, you can hang out at my place. My folks are taking a long weekend at some health spa for their anniversary. It'll just be me and Janie until Sunday."

We walked into the dark theater and waited for our eyes to adjust. I always thought that was pretty cool, how for a while you can't see anything, and then suddenly you can see pretty well. Like you're blind and then you're not.

"Perfect, the good seats are open," I said, pointing to the middle of the theater. "Thirteen rows from the front, right in the middle. That's the best sound."

Kaylee followed me, asking, "How do you know?"

"Oh, everyone knows," I said with a yawn. "They did a study with bats. Bats have great hearing, so they put bats in every seat in a theater and played the movie sound really low. Only the bats in the thirteenth row center got up and flew away."

"You're not serious," Kaylee said.

"You're right, I'm not," I admitted. "But thirteen is my favorite number."

We plopped down just in time for the preview. I like the movie previews as much as the movies because they show you all the best stuff. With some movies, if you see the preview, you don't even need to watch the movie.

The screen lit up and we saw what they call a typical neighborhood—you know, the kind where no one really lives but that the movie people think is real. There were kids playing hopscotch and jumping rope, someone washing a dog, all that stuff. Then, in the distance, there was a giant boom.

An announcer with a huge, deep voice said, *"Next summer . . ."*

More booms. The perfect neighborhood began to shake as if there was an earthquake.

Announcer: *". . . Just when you thought it was safe to go into the backyard . . . there's a new neighbor in town . . ."*

A giant sneaker stomped on someone's sport utility vehicle.

"That's one unhappy soccer mom," I whispered.

On the screen, a huge shadow fell over a dad barbecuing in his backyard. The dad looked up, and up, and said, "We're gonna need a bigger barbecue. . . ."

Suddenly three words whizzed onto the screen.

BIG

FAT

LIAR

Then a giant hand came down and wiped the words away. The screen went dark.

"Huh," Kaylee said with mild interest. "What do you think, you want to see it next summer?"

What I wanted, at that moment, was to puke.

"Jase? You want to see it?"

"See it!" I said. My voice sounded like a shriek. "See it? I wrote it!"

I guarantee you that if I'd had to race Superman or the Flash to get home to my house, I would have beaten both of them by at least a block. No contest.

When I got there, I did a quick check on the Internet, where you can find about a billion things you don't want and one or two things you do. Then I ran upstairs. My mom was in my parents' room packing her suitcase for the trip. She always did stuff like that with the TV on, and it was playing in the background when I burst in and started spilling the beans about *Big Fat Liar*. I'm not sure how much my mom actually heard, because I wasn't sure exactly what I said—it all came out pretty fast.

But when I stopped, Mom looked at me and said, "Are you trying to ruin your father's and my second honeymoon? Is that it?"

I swallowed a couple of big gulps of air. "I'm

telling you, I read about the plot of the movie on the Internet."

"What does that prove?" my mom asked. I don't think she or Dad had forgiven me for the whole summer school thing.

"It's exactly the same as my story!" I declared. "This guy lies to everyone in his town, until his girl-friend, who's this scientist, slips him this green liquid stuff that makes him bigger and bigger every time he tells a lie."

My mom rolled her eyes and turned toward the big walk-in closet. My dad was walking out at the same time, carrying a fistful of socks. At that moment the television announcer mentioned the phrase "big fat liar" and I stopped. The show on TV was *Inside Hollywood* or something like that, and they were running the teaser for *Big Fat Liar.*

The announcer, a guy named Pat who smiled at everything, said, "*Big Fat Liar* is already being touted as next summer's must-see movie event. With us in the studio is Marty Wolf, the mastermind behind this sure-to-be blockbuster."

The television screen widened to show Marty Wolf.

"That's him!" I shouted. "That's the guy from the limo!"

On TV, Pat said, "Marty, looks like you have a big hit on your hands with this one."

Marty Wolf looked pretty smug. "I'll tell you, Pat, we're ready to hit *BFL* out of the park. We're close to signing a very significant A-list star for the lead role of Kenny Trooper."

"Kenny Trooper!" I yelled at my parents. "See! I named him after our dog!"

Pat, all smiles, said, "Where in the world did you come up with this idea?"

Wolf shrugged. "Some ideas you struggle and struggle with. But the greats, well, they just seem to fall into your lap."

"Yeah, out of my backpack, you loser!" I shouted.

"Jason!" my parents said at the same time, with the same annoyed tone in their voices.

I looked at my dad. "Dad, I'm serious. That guy stole my paper. You have to believe me."

Well, I guess he *didn't* have to. Because he didn't.

9

nine

The only reason I didn't wake up early the next morning was because I never fell asleep. I tossed and turned all night, trying to figure out what to do. Not only had that guy stolen my story, but he was the reason I was stuck in summer school *and* the reason my parents didn't trust me anymore. I wasn't going to let Marty Wolf get away with it.

As soon as I heard my parents shuffling around downstairs, I threw off the covers and went down to greet them. After a quick "Good morning," my mom launched into a mission status report for my sister, Janie, who pretended to be listening. "The fridge is full. You've got our number in Arizona if you need us and . . . let's see, what else. Look, keep an eye on Jason, okay? You've got to be the parent for a few days, all right?"

Janie nodded, looking like a serious child-care provider. "I won't let him out of my sight, Mom."

They hugged; then my mom hugged me. A car horn honked outside. "Harry!" my mom called. "The car's here!"

My dad came rushing down and hugged each of us. He gave me a serious look. "I want you to forget about this Big Bad Liar business, okay?"

"Big *Fat* Liar," I corrected. "Which is what that guy is. He stole my story, Dad."

"Enough's enough!" my dad said. He nearly lost his cool, which is something my dad has never done, not even after the time I called his office and told them he'd quit so he could take me to a miniature golf course. "Jason, what did I tell you about trust? If you want us to start believing you again, don't claim you wrote some Hollywood movie. Work your tail off in summer school and make us proud. Okay?"

He snatched up his luggage and walked out the door. Both my parents stopped at the taxi to turn and wave one more goodbye. Then they were gone.

No sooner had the taxi left the curb than another car pulled up. This was an Isuzu Amigo in some bright neon color you'd never see in nature.

Janie's mom-in-the-making mood vanished. "Okay, Jase, I'll see you later. I'm going to Rudy's."

The car stopped at the curb.

"Who's Rudy?" I asked.

A teenage guy about my sister's age jumped out of the car and walked up to the door. He was dressed in baggy pants, an oversized baseball jersey, and a red baseball cap turned backward.

"He looks like he escaped from MTV," I whispered.

Rudy grabbed my hand and gave me one of those hip-hop handshakes that end in a hug. For a minute I thought he was attacking me, but then he thumped his chest and said, "Yo, wassup, dog?"

Janie smiled. "Jase, make yourself dinner, okay? We'll be back later."

Rudy tapped two fingers over his heart. "Peace out, little G." Then they both got into the car and drove off.

At any other time I would have been worried about my sister hanging out with the Vanilla Ice wannabe, but the truth was, it fit right into my plan.

I ran the three blocks to Kaylee's house. We've been friends for a long time, so it was no problem to walk around the side and through the back door. Kaylee was sitting at her kitchen table with another kid. They were looking down at a book and Kaylee was saying, "He's not literally a catcher eating rye bread. That's more like a metaphor for his adolescent angst."

"Angst?" said the other kid in a voice I recognized oh so well. "What's that, like pimples?"

"Kaylee, we've got to talk," I said.

"I'm tutoring," Kaylee said.

The guy she was tutoring turned around and it was (who else?) Bret Callaway. Bret noticed that I was out of breath from running and said, "Bet you wish you had your scooter, huh, Shepherd?"

I held my hands up like they were weight scales and said, "Hmm, let's see. Fully developed brain or Razor scooter. I think I'll take the brain." I looked at Kaylee. "Please. Pack your bags. We're going on a trip."

"Excuse me?" she asked.

"Can we talk in private?" I asked.

"No prob," Bret said. "I gotta take a dump anyway." He lumbered off.

As fast as I could, I told Kaylee about the plan I'd formed last night. It sounded simple in my head, but I admit that it came out a little more complicated when I said it out loud. I planned to fly to Los Angeles and make a megaproducer named Marty Wolf admit he'd stolen my story.

"You're crazy," Kaylee said. "I can't just go to Los Angeles."

"And I can't go through life having my parents think I'm a liar."

"But you are a liar!"

I paused. "Generally, that's true. But this one time I'm telling the truth. I wrote that paper, Kaylee, and I'm not going to rest until Wolf admits he stole it."

Kaylee started listing the reasons why we couldn't go. "What are we supposed to do, walk across the country?"

I grinned and held up a wad of cash. "Three years of yard work and baby-sitting money. Our flight leaves in two hours." I had booked it in the middle of the night.

"What about my grandma Pearl?" Kaylee pointed out. "I'm staying at her house while my parents are away."

I scowled. "That woman doesn't even know what year it is. Anyway, we'll be back by Sunday. I thought you wanted an adventure."

"I do, but, Jason, my grandma'll notice if I don't even show up at all."

That part I hadn't figured out yet. But the moment she asked, we heard Bret's voice from the other room. "Uh, Kaylee, you got a plunger? Someone clogged the toilet!"

Now I had that part figured out.

• • •

A half hour later, Kaylee, Bret, and I were standing at the door of Grandma Pearl's house. Bret was dressed in one of Kaylee's angora sweaters and a skirt. And he looked angry.

"I swear, Shepherd," he growled. "If any of my teammates see me, you're dead."

I tried to calm him down. "Hey, we made a deal. You want us to do your summer school homework or not?"

"Yeah, but . . ."

"It's just a few days," I reminded him. "And remember, you have to make your voice sound like a girl's."

Kaylee rang the bell, and she and I ducked behind an old bench on Grandma Pearl's porch. A second later the door opened and there stood Grandma herself. She was about four feet, nine inches tall, and she wore glasses so big and so thick that NASA could have used them as telescopes.

"Who's there?" Grandma Pearl snapped. "I have a gun!"

Bret didn't even try to disguise his voice. "Uh, it's Kaylee, Grandma."

Grandma Pearl smiled and showed her brown teeth—at least, all the ones she had left—and gave Bret a big hug. "Kaylee!" Then she paused and squeezed Bret's arms through the sweater. "Kaylee, you've gotten so tall. And muscular!"

Bret nodded. "Yeah, I'm benching like two-twenty, two-thirty."

Grandma Pearl smiled again and pulled him inside the house.

I heaved a sigh of relief. My plan was coming together.

10
ten

Airlines don't bother you if you're over twelve years old, so Kaylee and I didn't have any trouble getting on the plane or getting off at the Los Angeles International Airport. That was another part of my plan that worked perfectly.

The only problem was, I didn't have a plan after that.

We picked up our luggage and started walking toward the signs that said GROUND TRANSPORTATION. I wasn't sure what we would do or how we would find Marty Wolf. As we got near the exit doors, I saw several men holding up signs, waiting for passengers, and I got an idea.

I walked up to a guy dressed like the other limo driver I'd met. This guy was in his mid-twenties and had a nice-looking face. He was holding a sign that said MR. GARGANUS on it.

"I'm Mr. Garganus," I said.

The limo driver stared back at me. "You serious?"

I met his stare evenly. "Is there a problem?"

The limo driver shrugged. "Uh . . . no . . . it's just you're kind of young to be the Fur Coat King of the South."

Inwardly, I winced. Leave it to me to pick the name of some old tycoon. Well, that's one of the things about lying. Once you start, you've got to keep going with it. "Yeah, well, youth is a state of mind," I said. "I've been selling pelts since I was a baby."

The limo driver looked me over one more time. Then he shrugged. "All right. Well, I'm Frank."

"Frank, this is my associate, Kaylee. Now, Frank, take us to Universal Studios. We want to get in a little sightseeing before we start covering this town in fur."

Frank's long black limo was waiting out at the white curb. We got in and zipped away, leaving, I imagine, the real Fur Coat King out in the cold.

Okay, so somewhere in the back of my mind I was scared. Here I was, a fourteen-year-old kid in one of the biggest cities in the world without my parents knowing it, having dragged along my best friend. I admit—it nagged me. But that was deep down. On the surface, I was blown away by what we'd done. We rolled back the sunroof and stuck our heads out the top as the limo rolled through Beverly Hills, up Rodeo Drive, past the mansions of movie stars, then through Hollywood to Universal Studios.

Frank the limo driver dropped us off right at the front entrance to the Universal Studios theme park. "Thanks for the lift, Frank," I said. "We'll take it from here."

Frank grinned. He seemed to like us. We were probably different from the usual snooty passengers he picked up. "You got it, Mr. G. Here's my business card. Give me a shout any time you need a ride."

I took the card and saluted Frank. Then Kaylee and I walked up to the ticket window and bought our way onto the lot.

Universal Studios is pretty cool. It's an amusement park, with a ride that takes you past the shark from *Jaws*, through a fake avalanche, right alongside King Kong, and other stuff from the movies. But it's also a real, working movie studio, which means that in some parts of this gigantic place, people are filming real movies. And real producers have their offices there. That's the part that interested me most.

We bought tickets for the main tour and hopped onto a tram with a bunch of other tourists. As we whizzed off, the driver began to make comments on all the different sights we saw.

"So what's the plan?" Kaylee finally asked.

I said, "Well . . . this tram is bound to take us near Marty Wolf's building. When we get there, we jump off, infiltrate his office, and make Wolf admit he stole my paper."

Kaylee waited. Then she said, "That's it? That's the lamest plan I've ever heard."

"Trust me, it's gonna work," I said. But even *I* thought I was lying about that one.

The tour was cool. I could have sworn King Kong was going to rip off my head, and Kaylee nearly jumped out of her skin when the shark appeared about three inches from our tram. After that, the tram whisked us onto the back lot, where the movies were filmed. The tram driver said, "And this is the back lot, where many of our hit movies are filmed. To your left is the set for producer Marty Wolf's surefire summer smash *Big Fat Liar*. And right next to it is Mr. Wolf's office."

There it was. Enemy territory. I glanced at Kaylee, who nodded. The tram driver pointed to the opposite side of the tram, and we slipped off.

Walking across the lot was different from riding

in the tram. The people stopped looking like parts of an amusement park ride and suddenly seemed like real people doing real jobs. There were production assistants pushing racks of costumes, executives riding by on carts and talking on cell phones. There were even a few actors getting ready for their scenes.

We walked up to Marty Wolf's building and went into the lobby of Wolf Pictures. At a desk sat a receptionist. She wore a name tag that said ASTRID BARKER and a look that warned visitors that she was more watchdog than phone person.

"Can I help you?" she asked.

I said simply, "Yes, we're here to see Marty Wolf."

"Do you have an appointment?"

I sighed. "I ask you, Astrid. What kind of sick world is it when children need an appointment to see their own father?"

Astrid didn't even blink. "Mr. Wolf doesn't have children."

I shook my finger. "Not that he knows of. Look, this is going to be an emotional reunion for all of us. So once you let us in, you'll probably want to hold Papa's calls as well."

Astrid never cracked. "Mr. Wolf doesn't see anyone without an appointment." Her phone rang. She turned away from us. "Wolf Pictures."

Okay, so I bombed. It happens to the best of us. But the best don't give up. I glanced at Astrid's desk and spotted her car keys on a ring. The car keys were for a Honda, and the keychain was a little plastic picture frame with a photo of dear old Astrid with five poodles on her lap.

We walked across the lobby and I spotted an empty room with a bunch of copy machines in it. Inside, we found a phone extension. I gave Kaylee my latest idea—just invented—and she picked up the phone and dialed 0.

"Hi, Marty Wolf Pictures, please," she said.

The phone rang, and we could hear Astrid across the lobby. "Wolf Pictures."

Kaylee said, "Astrid Barker, please."

"Speaking."

"This is Doris Del Rio down in parking. Do you drive a Honda, ma'am?"

"Yes."

"Well, it's um . . ." Kaylee hesitated. I had to prompt her.

"It's parked on a dog," I whispered.

Kaylee covered the phone and hissed, "I'm not going to say that."

"Trust me!" I said.

Kaylee gulped and uncovered the phone. "Um, your car is . . . your car is parked on a dog, ma'am."

Outside and across the lobby, I could hear the tiniest hint of emotion creep into icy Astrid's voice. "My car is parked on a dog?" *Crack*.

"Yes, ma'am," Kaylee said. "In the tail area, to be more specific. It's awful. Listen for yourself."

She jabbed the phone at me. That caught me off guard. I started to whimper like a little poodle. We suddenly heard the phone slam down. I glanced out into the lobby just in time to see Astrid sprint for the door. She was pretty fast.

I grinned at Kaylee. "I don't know, Kaylee, you're more skilled than you think in the dark arts."

"Voodoo?" Kaylee asked.

"No, lying," I replied.

We marched across the lobby and I pointed to Astrid's desk. Kaylee sat down. "Keep a lookout," I said. "I'm sure this thing'll be over in a few minutes."

The phone rang and Kaylee picked it up. She looked nervous, but I could also tell she was enjoying this gag. I guess it was good to take a break from the straightlaced stuff now and then.

"Wolf Pictures," she said, answering a line. "I'm sorry, Mr. Wolf is about to go into a meeting. Can I take a message?"

I didn't wait to hear what the message was. I went down the hall to a big glass door. On the other side I could see a huge office and Marty Wolf himself, along with a young-looking woman who I'd soon learn was Monty, his personal assistant. Wolf was yelling so loudly I could hear him through the door.

"We're not just looking for my personal organizer, Monty. That thing is my life! So if you lost it, then you've killed me. Simple as that. Draw a line of chalk around me, baby, because I am dead!"

"I understand that," Monty said in a patient voice.

"No, you don't!" Wolf pouted.

I opened the door. "Um, excuse me?"

"Did you check your jacket pocket?" Monty asked.

Wolf fumed. "What do I look like, a moron? Of course I checked my jacket pocket. I always check my jacket pocket." He checked his jacket pocket. "Oh, it's in there."

He pulled out a slim electronic organizer called a Compaq iPAQ. Very cool, I had to admit. He tossed it on the desk.

"Excuse me," I said more loudly. "How's it going?"

Wolf finally noticed me. "Who are you?" he demanded.

"I'm Jason Shepherd," I said. "Remember me? I wrote *Big Fat Liar*."

Wolf's jaw dropped. I swear it nearly hit the

floor. "Uh, Monty, hold my calls. Give me a few minutes with Mr., uh, Mr. Shepherd here."

Monty gave me a long look. She had nice friendly eyes. They were clear, too. I had a feeling she saw through a lot of things, and I wondered if she saw through Wolf. Then she walked out. As the glass door closed behind her, Wolf pointed a remote at it, and the glass suddenly frosted over. There was no way to see through it.

Wolf sat down behind his desk and stared at me like I was a sideshow attraction. "Jason Shepherd. The young man from Greenbury, Michigan, right? I must tell you this is quite a surprise. What can I do for you, my friend?"

I said, "I want you to call my dad and tell him you stole my story that day in the limo."

"Call your dad?" Wolf said. He looked confused. "Why?"

"Because it's the truth and you're the only person he'll believe."

This seemed pretty straightforward. I mean, I may be a big fat liar sometimes, but I figured I'd give the truth a try. See if it worked.

Wolf leaned forward. "You mean you traveled halfway across the country to get me to call your dad and tell him you did your homework?"

"Yup. You make that call, and you'll never hear from me again."

He stared at me for a minute longer. I couldn't tell what he was thinking. Finally, he said, "Okay."

Well, that was easy, I thought.

Wolf got up and went over to a safe in the wall. He dialed a combination and opened it up. "What are you doing?" I asked.

"I'm getting the story. It's a great piece of work. I refer to it whenever I get in a bind on the script."

He returned to his desk and dropped the story down right in between us. I was surprised. I'd thought it would be harder to convince him, but I wasn't complaining. "So you'll give it back to me and make the phone call?"

Wolf nodded. "You gave me my movie, Shepherd. It's the least I can do. You smoke cigars?"

I frowned at him. "I'm fourteen, Wolf."

"Right, of course, of course," Wolf said. He opened a small case on his desk and pulled out a cigar. He cut off the tip. "You know, whenever I close a deal, I like to celebrate with a fine cigar. Jason, it was a pleasure doing business with you."

He lit a match and started puffing on his cigar. Suddenly he dropped the match. I watched it fall right onto my story. "Oh, ah, oh my, oh no, what have I done?" he said without meaning a word of it.

"No!" I yelled.

I reached out to grab the story, but Wolf pulled it away, jabbing at the pages as though he was trying to put out the fire. What he was really doing was poking more holes in some pages and igniting other ones with the hot end of the cigar.

"I'll get water!" he said. Wolf ran over to a minibar against the wall, snatched up a bottle of clear liquid, and poured it on the pages. The fire flared up, and the pages vanished.

Wolf stared at the smoldering ashes. "What a tragedy. The last piece of evidence that proves I stole *BFL* from you gone up in smoke."

I stared at him for a moment. That was the first time I realized that I was dealing with someone seriously twisted. I mean, I've told a lie or two, but this guy was genuinely nuts. "You're sick, you know that?"

Wolf considered it. "I've definitely got some issues to work out. But come on, kid, I'm Marty Wolf, the Human Hit Factory. I've got a reputation to keep up. You really think I'd admit to anyone that your little story became the movie that's going to save my career?"

I snatched up his phone and jabbed it at him. "I don't care about your movie. I just want you to call my dad and tell him I wrote that paper."

Wolf laughed. "Or else what? You'll shoot me

71

with a spitball? Grow up, Shepherd. This is Hollywood, baby. It's a dog-eat-dog town. Worse! You got cats eating cats, fish munching on fish. We play by our own rules out here."

Wolf went over to close his safe. As he did, I looked around, desperate for some way to convince him. My eyes landed right on his iPAQ.

Wolf came back to the desk. "Okay, I'm making a call, all right." He dialed a couple of numbers and said, "Hey, Rocco, this is the Wolf. Send a couple of your boys down here. I got a Code W. Another angry writer refusing to leave."

I gave him my best snarl. "I tried to play fair, Wolf. But you asked for it."

The glass door opened and two tough-looking security guards walked in. "Meeting's over, Shakespeare," Wolf said dismissively.

The two guards grabbed me by the arms and turned me toward the door. As we walked out, I saw Monty walk in. She glanced at me, then at the pile of ashes near the desk, and then at Marty Wolf.

The guards walked me to the lobby, where I saw Kaylee still taking phone calls. She looked like an old pro. As I was dragged out, Astrid the receptionist dragged herself back in. Kaylee jumped up and handed a message sheet to the confused woman.

"Hey, Astrid. Adam Sandler called to set up a

lunch. I sent flowers to Meg Ryan 'cause she sounded like she had a cold. Oh, and I did some reorganizing. Your drawers were a total mess."

By the time Kaylee caught up to me, I was sitting on the curb outside Wolf's building, fuming. I think she thought I was mad, but the truth was, I was planning.

"So, that went well, huh?" she said sarcastically.

"This is Hollywood, Kaylee," I said. "It's a fish-eat-fish town. They play by their own rules."

"Does that mean we're going home?"

I nodded. "Yep, just as soon as Wolf admits the truth."

Kaylee frowned. "I'm not trying to go all negative on you, Jase, but didn't Marty Wolf just turn you down flat?"

"He'll do it," I said.

"Why?"

I grinned. I admit, I'd been waiting for the right moment to open my fist. In it was Marty Wolf's iPAQ. "Because I've got his life in the palm of my hand."

Instead of being impressed, Kaylee looked like I'd just shown her someone's small intestine. "Great. We're stealing now."

"Not stealing," I protested. "We're borrowing." I started to go through the iPAQ. It really was a cool machine. "Look, we've got Wolf's alarm codes, credit card numbers, his schedule . . ."

"So?"

"So, I'm sure we can figure out some way to use all this info against him."

"I don't know . . ."

"Give me one day to come up with a plan," I pleaded. "I can't go home unless my dad knows the truth."

Kaylee stared at me for about as long as Wolf had. But her look was different. Hers was the look of a friend who wanted to help me, but I could tell that she wasn't sure helping meant dragging me back home or staying here. Finally, she said, "Do you think your plan might include food and a place to sleep?"

As a matter of fact, it did.

On the way to Wolf's office, I'd seen a building marked NO TRESPASSING. The funny thing about signs like that is that if everyone follows them, no one ever goes inside . . . which means the building must be empty. One of the doors was open, so I slipped inside with Kaylee right behind me. Inside, we saw a huge warehouse full of old props, clothes, and other stuff they used to make movies. There was dust everywhere. Obviously, no one came here often.

"Looks like we found our temporary," I said. I yawned. "Let's get some shut-eye, K. Tomorrow we begin Phase One. Surveillance."

11
eleven

So either I had a very elaborate, highly organized plan for getting my revenge on Marty Wolf, or I was making it up as I went along.

You know me by now. You guess which one it was.

We had a pretty good night's sleep, thanks to about two dozen fake furs that made two great beds. The next morning, I fired up my cell phone and pulled out the card of Frank the limo driver. One call and I said, "Hey, Frank. Mr. Garganus here. We'll meet you in front of the studio in twenty minutes."

Kaylee and I hurried to the front gates just as the limo was pulling up. We hopped into the backseat and I said, "Morning, Frank. Let's get moving. We've got furs to sell."

Frank turned around, and this time his friendly face wasn't so friendly. "Fur Coat King of the South, my behind. You almost cost me my job, you little weasel. You owe me a hundred bucks for yesterday's ride."

I gulped. I guess the real Fur Coat King of the South had been upset when his ride never showed. "Frank, look, I can explain."

"I don't want an explanation. I want a hundred dollars. And I want you out of my limo."

"I . . . I . . ." The weird thing was, the more I needed to be lying, the worse I was getting at it. "Look, I'm sorry," I said at last. "We came here to see this guy, Marty Wolf. He stole something from me—"

"Did you just say Marty Wolf?" Frank asked. He looked totally shocked.

"Yeah. You know him?"

"Know him? I used to drive him. He fired me last year."

"I don't believe this," Kaylee said (like I'd never heard those words before).

"Why'd he fire you?" I asked.

"I'm an actor. I made the mistake of asking him if I could ever audition for one of his movies. He could have just said no, but he took one of my audition pictures and wrote 'Loser' across the top and faxed it to every director in town. The guy totally ruined my confidence."

"That's terrible," I said.

Frank nodded. "I haven't even tried to get an audition in months. If you want to mess with Wolf, I'll help you out any way I can."

I told you a lot of this might sound unbelievable, but there you have it.

While we were smoothing things over with Frank the limo driver, Marty Wolf was waking up in his Beverly Hills mansion. As he rolled over, he stared at a ratty old stuffed animal, a monkey. He said, "It's showtime, Mr. Funnybones," which was sort of his morning ritual. Then he got up, pulled on a swimsuit, and went out to his pool.

According to his iPAQ, Marty Wolf swam every morning.

His iPAQ also said he had a meeting at his office at 9 A.M., but he was late. Kaylee and I watched him roll up to the gate in his BMW at 9:25. The gate guard was out of his little guardhouse, and Wolf honked impatiently. A minute later, the guard—a tubby guy with a face like a nice old grandfather and a name tag that read LEO—waddled out of a service room.

He smiled at Wolf and said, "Sorry, Mr. Wolf, nature called. My wife made a casserole last night. The thing's shooting through me like a cannonball."

Wolf glared at him. "I'd love to sit here and talk about your digestive tract, but instead, could you do me a favor and *open the gate, you chunky loser*!"

Leo's face fell. Blushing, he pushed a button, and the gate opened up. I felt sorry for him, but at least he was too upset to notice as Kaylee and I slipped through the gate behind Wolf's car. We hustled across the lot to his office and snuck around the back. There was a window in his office, and we sat under it hidden by the bushes, listening in as Wolf walked in on a meeting with some of his crew.

"Sorry I'm late, people!" he said, lying through his teeth. "A bus hit a truck carrying horses. I'm not going to go into details. It was awful. There were hooves. . . . Anyway . . ." He got down to business. "We start production in two days. Dusty, first up is the big stunt. I want to start the shoot off with a bang."

He looked at a Chinese man who must have been the director. Dusty spoke in a heavy Chinese accent, but he looked very excited about his job. "I ready to party! I shoot stunt from twelve different camera angle . . . with smoke and birds flying everywhere."

Wolf held up his hands. "Whoa, whoa, easy does

it! I can barely afford one camera, let alone twelve. And you can forget about the birds, too." He looked at Monty. "Talk to me about the budget."

Monty checked her clipboard. "We're two million dollars over and we haven't shot one scene yet. The studio hasn't approved the new budget."

"When are they supposed to do that?" Wolf asked.

"Tomorrow morning. You have a breakfast meeting at Duncan Ross's house."

Wolf scoffed, plopped into his chair, and put his feet up. "Yeah, right. Tell our little vice president that he can drag his butt over to my place if he wants to have a sit-down with the Wolfster."

Monty tossed a copy of *Variety* onto the desk. On the top page was a story about Duncan Ross. "Actually, sir, he's not a VP anymore."

Wolf glanced at the article, which started with the headline DUNCAN ROSS PROMOTED TO STUDIO PRESIDENT. He scowled. "I see. Well, uh . . . get directions then. Don't want to be late, now, do we?"

Wolf glanced around at his crew. "Now, for the big stunt, I want serious media coverage. TV, print, that Internet stuff, everything. I need a hit, people. I gotta get the buzz going early. Who's handling that?"

A large woman with really big jowls lifted her meaty hand off the table. "I am. Jocelyn Davis. Senior VP of publicity."

Wolf looked her over. "You sure you're not the senior VP of Twinkies?"

Jocelyn gave him a cold stare, but all she said was "I'll make sure the shoot is well covered."

Wolf slapped his hands on the table. "Terrific. Okay, people, meeting's over." He looked at Jocelyn. "I guess you can sing now. What's next?"

What was next, according to Wolf's iPAQ, was the rehearsal for the big stunt. Thanks to the notes, we got there ahead of Wolf himself. It was a four-story building on the studio lot where they did a lot of special stunts. Kaylee and I climbed the stairs of a building next to the one they were using, and we had a perfect view of everything that happened.

Wolf showed up with his entourage just as the stunt guys were getting set. They'd blown up a huge air bag about forty feet below a big window. Wolf, Monty, and some other movie flunkies were standing around the air bag, along with a guy we guessed was the stunt coordinator. Everyone called him Vince, and he looked the way I figured a stuntman should look. Tan, tough, sharp blue eyes. He was older—maybe sixty—but his white hair was thick. He looked like the kind of guy you'd want flying your airplane if it started to go down.

Suddenly a man came flying through the window, cartwheeling through the air, and landed safely in the air bag. Everyone applauded, and Vince helped the stuntman up from the crash bag.

"What do you think, Marty?" Vince asked.

Wolf said, "Yeah, it's perfect. The only thing is I liked it better the first time I saw it . . . in 1942, you freakin' dinosaur!"

Vince was so shocked he took a step back. Wolf pointed to one of his team members, a nerdy guy with a thin beard. "Vince, meet my new effects whiz, Lester Golub. He's gonna create the stunt on his iMac, and your stunt guy's going to do exactly what the computer tells him."

Vince frowned like a trusted soldier who's been retired. "I don't need a computer to show me how to do my job."

Wolf was still looking at Lester. "Geek-Boy, ignore Father Time over here. From the looks of you, I'm sure you don't have a social life, so you two will meet up tomorrow to finalize the details."

A hurt look came into Lester's eyes, but he didn't say anything. Vince, however, wasn't so shy. "I'm off tomorrow. Personal day. I'm taking my granddaughter to a birthday party."

Vince pulled a card out of his jacket pocket and

held it up. It was shaped like a little clown in blue and orange.

"I like Vince," Kaylee whispered from our hideaway. "He's a good guy."

"Yeah," I said. "He's the sergeant in the war movie who you hope doesn't get shot down at the end."

Wolf read the clown card. "Nice. Kid party in Beverly Hills. Looks like fun." Suddenly his voice rose in pitch. *"Well, I got news for you, Grandpa, this is Hollywood! You can rest when you're dead!"*

He snatched the clown card away and ripped it.

I shook my head. "Wolf, on the other hand, is the evil dictator who needs to have a missile dropped down his chimney."

Kaylee asked the obvious question. "How are we going to do that?"

For a minute I didn't know what to say. Then I looked down below, where Marty Wolf was turning his back on Vince the stunt coordinator. I watched the pieces of the clown invitation flutter to the ground. And then I knew exactly how to bring Marty Wolf down.

12
twelve

I liked our headquarters. Someone else might have thought of it as a dusty warehouse, but to me it was the Batcave, our Fortress of Solitude, our secret base under Mt. Rushmore.

It was also full of cool stuff, which helped. In the middle of the room was an enormous *T. rex* with very lifelike claws and eyes. On one side of the warehouse Kaylee found an entire wall of Velcro. She strapped Velcro strips to her arms and legs and threw herself up against the wall.

Meanwhile, I was deep in thought, smoothing out the wrinkles in my plan. Totally focused. And playing pinball, too. But, hey, even a genius has to take a coffee break now and then, right?

My cell phone rang, startling me so badly that I nearly dropped it. "H-hello?" I said.

"Hey, Jase!" My father. I could barely hear him over the *ping-ping*s of the pinball machine. "Just called to see how you're doing."

I looked around the warehouse. Suddenly, the *T. rex* seemed to be staring directly at me. "Uh, Dad! Fine. You know, studying really hard. Staying out of, um, trouble."

"Good, good. What's that noise?" he asked.

I knew what he meant. The minute I'd said the word *Dad,* Kaylee had frozen. But the pinball machine was still chiming and dinging like I'd just won a jackpot. I tried to muffle the sound, but it was too loud. "Oh, it's an experiment for my science class. I'm doing some work with ball bearings. It's a gravity thing."

Yikes. I'd snuck away to Hollywood to prove to my dad that I *wasn't* a liar.

"Sounds good," he said, which made me feel bad, "sounds good. Anyway, I just wanted to check in because you looked pretty upset when we left."

"Yeah, well, about that, Dad. I just want you to know, I totally get what you said about the whole trust thing. And I think when you get back, you'll see that I've been trying really hard to earn it."

Well, *that* was true.

My dad's voice sounded warm and even a little proud. "I'm glad to hear it, pal. We love you, and we'll see you in a couple of days."

"Good night, Dad."

I clicked my phone off and looked at Kaylee, who had stayed Velcro'd to the wall, not wanting to make any noise my dad would hear. "You've got to love cell phones. My dad calls and thinks I'm at home." I smiled at Kaylee, who was stuck sideways to the wall. "By the way, thanks for keeping so still."

Kaylee strained but couldn't budge herself. "I wasn't . . . doing it . . . for you. Little help here?"

I laughed. Grabbing her hands, I pulled hard. There was a huge ripping sound that I hoped wasn't her arms coming out of their sockets, and she popped off the Velcro wall.

"Thanks," she said.

"Uh, really, thank you," I said back. I looked at her for a minute, but her eyes were a little too bright and pretty for me and I didn't want to go all soft and gushy, so I turned away. Kaylee is my best friend, and that's a special status you just don't mess with. But I have to admit I like her *a lot*. "Thanks for coming out here with me." I was pretty sure I blushed.

I was also pretty sure that Kaylee noticed. But

she didn't say anything. "I came for the adventure, remember."

There was nothing cooler than a girl who knew you were embarrassed and didn't make you feel even worse. "Anyway, I owe you one. But we have a big day tomorrow."

"What happens?"

I grinned. "Just a little ditty I like to call Phase Two."

So here's a thing you'll notice about people in Hollywood. A lot of them live all by themselves in houses that are much too big for them. They buy mansions designed to hold entire families and end up using only one or two rooms.

Marty Wolf was one of these people.

He woke up early the next morning when his alarm went off. It was custom-designed to play the theme from *Entertainment Tonight*. And just as he did first thing every morning, Marty smiled at an old, ratty stuffed monkey doll and said, "It's showtime, Mr. Funnybones."

The monkey just smiled back at him with its faded mouth.

Wolf got up, stretched, and put on a bathing suit, then stumbled downstairs and outside to his swimming pool.

As he went into the pool, Kaylee and I went into the house and started up the stairs. Kaylee's face looked as white as a sheet. "Great. Breaking and entering. Add that to our record."

I tried to calm her. "We didn't break. We just entered."

"Okay," she said, "but when people ask, you lured me here with your advanced mind-manipulation techniques."

Before coming to Wolf's house that morning (thanks to Frank the limo driver, who really had it in for the guy), we'd gathered together a few little household items. One of them was a bottle of Super Glue. As we snuck into Wolf's bedroom, I spotted his cell phone on the nightstand. Next to it was one of those earpieces with a cord attached. I dabbed a little Super Glue onto the earpiece and moved on.

Then we went to the shower. I poured the shampoo out of his shampoo bottle, and taking a bottle out of my little goody bag, I poured new liquid into the old bottle.

By the way, in case you're wondering, we had already poured a little something into Marty's pool water.

Seven o'clock. Laps. That's what the iPAQ said.

As we finished filling the bottle, we heard Wolf coming upstairs. We scrambled out of the bathroom and ducked behind the bed.

Wolf didn't know it yet, but he walked into his bedroom that morning a changed man.

He was blue.

We had spiked Wolf's pool water with blue dye, courtesy of a makeup locker in the studio warehouse. It was, in fact, the exact same shade of blue as the clown on the card Wolf had ripped up, and he had been soaking in it for the past fifteen minutes. Now his skin was a deep shade of blue. We could hear Wolf singing to himself as he went into his bathroom, opened the shower door, and started the water running. Then he got in and, a few minutes later, popped open the shampoo bottle and started to scrub.

I don't know if he even noticed that the stuff coming out of the bottle was orange. I don't know if he checked the bottle and saw that it was, according to the label, his usual brand of hair stuff.

All I know is that, a few minutes later, the shower water stopped, the door opened, and Wolf must have stepped out. That must have been when he finally looked at himself in the mirror, because a second later his house was filled with the loudest shriek of surprise I'd ever heard.

It was very satisfying.

13
thirteen

We could still hear him shrieking all the way from the limo.

"Mission accomplished?" Frank asked.

"So far, so good," I said, dropping the bag of goodies onto the backseat. "Never underestimate the power of a fourteen-year-old's pranks. Speaking of which . . ." I popped open my cell phone and handed it to Kaylee. "Can you work your magic one more time?"

Kaylee frowned. She definitely hadn't been happy about pouring the blue dye into Wolf's pool, and she had nearly gotten sick over sneaking into his house. Face it, Kaylee was a genuinely good person, and I was pushing her to her limit. "I don't know . . ."

"Please."

"Why don't you do it?" she asked.

"Because I don't have your talent for this!" I started dialing the number from the iPAQ and then handed the phone to her. She sighed.

The number I had dialed was the direct line for Marty Wolf's assistant, and we heard her say, "Wolf Pictures. This is Monty."

Kaylee took a deep breath and launched into a speech in a voice that was, like, totally right out of a teen flick. "Monty! Janine from Duncan Ross's office. Cookie, I'm soooo psyched you're there. I was watching *Charmed* on the WB last night, when, just as, like, Shannen Doherty was about to put a spell on Alyssa Milano, I had the biggest panic attack that I forgot to give you Duncan's new address!"

Over the phone, Monty said, "That was quick. I didn't know he moved."

"Ho-yeah," Kaylee said in her imitation-Hollywood voice. "In a big way. He bought, like, the slickest pad in 90210. We're talking mondo-bucks. Anyhoo, tell Mr. Wolf he lives at . . ."

And Kaylee proceeded to read off the address that had been written on the clown invitation.

I love it when a plan comes together.

Asking Kaylee to help me out of a tight spot.

Ms. Caldwell isn't happy with me. Again!

The mighty Marty Wolf.

Riding in style.

Wow! Universal Studios.

"Marty Wolf, please."

Wolf's "life" is in the palm of my hand.

Cool costumes from our secret hideout.

"It's showtime, Mr. Funnybones."

Wolf's shriek was music to my ears!

Planning Phase Three.

And on to Phase Four.

My plan was a success!

● ● ●

A few minutes later, Monty dialed Marty Wolf's cell phone. Even if he was home, the cell was usually the best place to reach him.

She caught him as he was heading down to his BMW. Marty Wolf was not a happy man. His hair was bright orange. His face was probably red with rage, but you couldn't tell because his skin was deep blue. When the phone rang, he stuck the earpiece in his ear and answered.

"It's Monty," said his assistant's voice. "I'm glad I caught you. Duncan moved. His new address is—"

"You've got to cancel the meeting!" Wolf interrupted. "And get one of the makeup chicks to meet me at the office. This is an emergency!"

"Marty, you can't miss this meeting. If Duncan doesn't approve the budget, we can't start shooting tomorrow."

"I don't think you understand, Monty," Wolf sputtered. "I'm blue!"

Monty's voice took on a soothing tone. "Hey, come on, Marty, we all get down sometimes . . ."

"No, no, no!" Wolf was about to burst a blood vessel. "I mean, I'm literally . . . and I've got orange . . ." he sputtered. "Forget it. Give me his address. I'll figure something out."

"Seven-sixty-seven North Maple."

Wolf slid into his car and closed the door. "Right. Have you come up with an ending for the script yet?"

"I'm working on it," Monty said uncomfortably. She always got anxious talking about writing, partly because she loved to write and wanted to do a good job, but also because Wolf always took the credit. "But I could use a little help, Marty."

Wolf snorted. "Monty, I am writing and producing a major motion picture. I don't have time to work on the script. That's your job. Now, stop wasting time and get to work! I'm twenty-four hours away from the most important shoot of my career!"

Wolf clicked off his phone and yanked the earpiece out of his ear. At least he tried to. But the Super Glue stuck fast. When he yanked the cord, he pulled his own head to the side and it smacked against the car window.

We followed Wolf on his drive through Bel-Air and Beverly Hills. He must have been glad he had his Beemer windows tinted so no one could see him. This was the richest area of Los Angeles, and all the major players in Hollywood lived around here. The last thing he would have wanted was to be seen with this weird dye job. Man, I bet he was planning a big fat lawsuit for that shampoo company!

Wolf pulled up to the address Monty had given him. It was a nice house in Beverly Hills, but not as big as he'd thought it would be. I mean, if he'd been Duncan Ross and he'd just been made president of a studio, he'd have gone all the way, baby. Mansion, guest mansion, tennis courts, the works. But this Ross guy was pretty straightlaced. He was probably putting all his money away for his retirement, the dweeb.

Wolf got out of his car and marched up to the door. I have to admit, he looked pretty confident despite his exotic coloring, although I don't know if he'd figured out an explanation yet. He knocked, and the door was opened by a housekeeper with a Spanish accent.

"Hi, I'm—"Wolf started to say.

But the housekeeper took one look at his blue skin and hair and said, *"Sí, sí.* They've been waiting for you." She grabbed his wrist and pulled him into the house quickly.

We saw Wolf feeling his pockets, probably looking for his iPAQ. *Fat chance!* I thought.

The housekeeper walked Wolf toward a set of double doors. "I must warn you, they like to play a little rough."

Wolf snorted. He could handle Duncan Ross. "Sister, I invented the word *rough*. Duncan'll be eating sugar cubes out of my hand by the time I'm finished with him."

"*¿Qué?*" the housekeeper said in Spanish.

"Let's go,"Wolf said.

The housekeeper shrugged and threw open the double doors. Wolf stomped in . . . and found himself in the midst of twenty nine-year-old kids armed with party favors, horns, hats, Silly String, and streamers.

"What the—?" he asked.

One kid, obviously the birthday boy, jumped to his feet and pointed a chubby finger at Wolf. "The clown's here!"

The other kids cheered.

"Let's hurt him!"

Wolf's eyes went as wide as saucers, which only made him look even more like a clown. The birthday boy jumped on him and two other kids dragged him to the ground. Wolf might have been in some knock-down, drag-out arguments in production meetings, but he'd never been attacked by a pack of wild elementary schoolers. They took him by surprise. But Hollywood certainly taught a person to fight dirty, and that's what Marty Wolf did. He put the birthday boy in a headlock and shouted, "Get off me, you psychos!"

But then someone pulled his hair and yet another little animal landed on him WWF-style.

Kaylee and I watched the commotion from outside the house. We weren't interested in Wolf anymore, just in his BMW. "Do you have the alarm code?" I asked.

Kaylee waved the iPAQ. "I'm all over it." She aimed the digital device at the Beemer. The car alarm chirped, and we jumped inside. I popped the glove compartment, pulled out the owner's manual, and skimmed through it.

"Don't you want to read it more?" Kaylee asked.

"Why?" I said with a grin. "We're not exactly trying to get anything right, so it doesn't really matter how wrong we are."

Kaylee thought about it for a minute. "I see your point."

We got to work.

My sources revealed the following scene happening inside the house. Wolf finally managed to break away from the pack. He was running toward the back door, fumbling with his cell phone. He managed to press the speed dial and heard Monty say "Hello" over the sound of screaming children.

"Where did you send me!" he shouted back. "You've got to get me out of here!"

"The meeting's not going well?" Monty asked. She heard screaming in the background, but screaming was a part of all Marty Wolf meetings, so it didn't faze her.

He shrieked, "No! They think I'm a clown!"

"I'm sure you're overreacting, Marty," Monty said. "Keep plugging away. This is important."

"DIE, CLOWN, DIE!"

Wolf whirled at the sound of the battle cry, just in time to see two kids in ninja costumes leap off the stairs. He ducked and they flew over him. Seeing his opening, Wolf dashed for the door and escaped into the backyard. Limping, with torn clothes, he jogged around to the front of the house.

"You don't get it, you don't get it!" he shouted at Monty. "It's the wrong house. It's a stupid kids' party, you idiot!"

Monty's back stiffened a little. "Take it easy, Marty. How was I supposed to know it was the wrong address? Between ghostwriting your movie, keeping track of the budget, looking for your orga-nizer—"

"Yeah, where is my freakin' iPAQ?" Wolf growled. "That thing is my life! I'm bleeding over here. You've got to get Duncan to reschedule."

"Already done," Monty said efficiently. "One o'clock at Duncan's office. And remember, you have the premiere of *Whitaker and Fowl* at five P.M. and the party at your house afterward."

Wolf got to his car and started to calm down. "Right, right. That's good. Yeah, we'll get Duncan to sign off on the *Big Fat Liar* budget and then blow him away with *Whitaker and Fowl.* Oh, and, Monty, you finish up those script pages, I might just let you leave the office early and come to the premiere."

Monty bit her lip. "Gee, thanks, Mr. Wolf," she said sarcastically.

Wolf cut off his cell phone. He got into his Beemer and drove away from the house. Rounding a turn, he put his foot on the brake and his horn honked, making him jump a foot off the seat. He flipped his blinker and the radio came on, blasting the tune "You're So Vain." When he tried to turn off the radio, the music kept playing but the trunk popped open.

"What's happening?" Wolf shouted. He eased up to a stop sign.

A black limousine rolled up next to him. The dark-tinted window slid down, and Marty Wolf found himself staring into the grinning face of yours truly.

"Hey, Wolf," I said. "I like your new coloring. It works for you."

Wolf's blue face turned purple, and I was pretty sure I saw steam coming out of his ears. "You . . . you did this?"

I nodded. "Yup. And it can end anytime. All you

have to do is make a phone call. Shouldn't be much of a problem, since that headset is Super Glued to your ear."

I leaned out the window and flicked a business card into Wolf's car. Then, right on cue, Frank put the limo in motion and we pulled away. Wolf must have tried to chase us, changing gears and hitting the accelerator, because suddenly every device in the BMW went off, lights flashing, horn blaring, windshield wipers whooshing, and water squirting everywhere.

A few blocks ahead, at a red light, Wolf's BMW zoomed up behind a gigantic monster truck with tires as big as a house. Wolf slammed on the brakes, making the horn blare. But the car came a stop without touching the big truck, and Wolf heaved a sigh of relief.

The old lady behind Wolf wasn't quite so fast. She was driving an old Cadillac convertible that was as big (and slow) as a boat. It bumped into Wolf's car, sending him forward so that his Beemer bumped up against the back fender of the monster truck. Wolf leaned out his window and snapped, "Get glasses, Grandma!"

This old lady, apparently, wasn't the type to take any guff. "Up yours, Blue Boy!" she shouted back.

But it wasn't the old lady Wolf should have been

worried about. The door of the monster truck opened up and the driver climbed out. He was a big guy with combed-back hair, wearing a mesh T-shirt and a shark-tooth necklace. He topped all that off with a zebra-striped sweat suit and the kind of scowl you can only get from chewing lots and lots of tobacco.

He lumbered around to the back of his truck, where he saw, only by squinting, the tiniest scratch. When he stood up, he was so angry that veins started popping out on his forehead.

"Oh my god! I'm gonna kill you!"

Wolf got out of his car, hands palm up. "It wasn't my fault. The old bag rear-ended me."

I guess the old lady was as smart as she was tough. She was already pulling away. But she managed to yell, "Eat my bloomers!" before burning rubber.

"You're gonna pay for this!" Zebra-Stripe growled. He ran back to his truck and climbed in. Wolf heard the engine rev, and then the truck lurched backward.

"No!" Wolf yelled, scrambling out of the way.

The big tires rolled up the front of the BMW, turning seventy-five-thousand dollars' worth of German engineering into scrap metal.

14
fourteen

Fast-forward to the office of Duncan Ross, studio president: 1:10 in the afternoon. Duncan sat there, staring across his big desk at Monty and, beside her, an empty chair.

Duncan checked his watch: 1:11.

"Two meetings in a row, Monty," he said in a low, ominous voice. "This is not the way to get on the new president's good side."

Monty nodded. "I'm sorry, sir. I'm sure there's an explanation. Um, well, would you like to take a look at the new script pages?"

Duncan thought about it and nodded. Monty slid some pages across the desk and sat back, clenching her fingers nervously. Duncan read through the pages without a change in expression. He might have been a statue. But then, at the end, the edges of his mouth turned up the slightest bit and he chuckled.

"That's good, Trooper's final line there," he rumbled. "Very funny."

Monty sighed, relieved. "Thank you, sir!" she said. Then she caught herself. "Oh, um, I mean, on behalf of Marty. I mean, he wrote it, of course."

"Hmm," Duncan said skeptically.

"I'll . . . let me try him again on his cell phone. Maybe he had car trouble."

At that moment, Marty Wolf was riding in the passenger seat of a tow truck. On a flatbed at the back of the tow truck sat what was left of his car— which now resembled nothing so much as a waste-paper basket with a hood ornament.

When his phone rang, Wolf clicked it on. "What!"

"It's Monty," she said softly. "Where are you? I'm sitting in Duncan's office!"

"I'm not going to make it," Wolf said, as though confessing something she didn't already know. "Tell him it was your fault and reschedule."

Monty stood up and casually turned away from Duncan. Into her phone, she whispered, "I'm not lying to the new president of the studio, Marty."

On his end of the connection, Wolf scowled. "Don't get all high and mighty on me, Monty, because if I go down, you're riding shotgun, Tootsie Roll. Now, make something up, and I'll smooth things over with him at the premiere."

Monty hesitated for the shortest moment, then surrendered. "Fine."

"And call Rocco Malone. I want him to find Jason Shepherd and have him thrown out of town. That kid is starting to really bother me."

Wolf and Monty hung up on each other.

Monty took a deep breath and turned to find Duncan Ross studying her closely. He was a nice man, she thought, looking back at him. And a smart man. But he wasn't a fool. You didn't have to be a genius to become president of a movie studio, but you did have to know how to read the people around you. She doubted she could fool him. But, she thought with a slight hint of misery, it was her job.

"Sir . . . I apologize. It was my fault. It seems I gave Mr. Wolf the wrong time for the meeting. He won't be able to make it."

Duncan Ross didn't respond. He just continued to study her with a look that seemed to see right through her.

15
fifteen

That evening just before five o'clock, a crowd began to gather outside the Cineramadome, a very cool theater. About twenty years ago, when my father was a kid, it must have looked futuristic, with a round shell that made it look like a globe and big dents all over that must have made it look like the moon.

Massive spotlights pointed up toward the sky, sweeping back and forth. A red carpet had been rolled out from the curb right up to the doors of the theater. A line of limousines stretched down the block, waiting to unload their cargoes of celebrities and movie executives who'd been invited to the premiere.

The crowd, the spotlights, the red carpet, the limos, and the celebrities were all there for the opening of Marty Wolf's latest picture, *Whitaker and Fowl.*

As one of the limos spilled its passengers, the crowd began to murmur. The new arrival was Jaleel White, the movie's costar. He sauntered up the red carpet, obviously pleased to be taken as a real actor now and not that dweeb Urkel.

Suddenly a reporter jumped onto the carpet and stuck a microphone under his chin. "Jaleel, any comment on the stories that you got into a fight with the chicken and threatened to eat him alive?"

"Yes," Jaleel said with a grin. "Those rumors are completely untrue. Whitaker and I got along great during the shoot. He was a pleasure to work with."

"This must be an exciting night for you," the reporter remarked.

Jaleel nodded. "I'm just glad to put the past behind me and finally be taken seriously as an actor. I deserve a little respect—"

"Oh my god, it's the chicken!" the reporter shrieked, pushing Jaleel aside and scrambling down the carpet.

Behind Jaleel, another limo rolled up and a

chicken hopped out, shooed there by a farmer who looked uncomfortable in the limelight. The chicken was wearing a little tuxedo and sunglasses. Camera flashes popped and voices rang out, shouting questions to the clucking bird. Jaleel waited a moment, then groaned and shook his head. Show business.

Near the entrance to the theater, a reporter was speaking into the lens of a camera, broadcasting back to a studio. "It seems like all of Hollywood has turned out for this one, but the question remains . . . where is Marty Wolf?"

I could have told him, because at that moment I was sitting across the street from the theater on a bus stop bench, watching a blue Los Angeles city bus roll to a stop. But I wasn't waiting to get on. I was waiting for someone to get off.

Sure enough, out limped Marty Wolf, still blue, still carrot-topped, and still wearing his torn suit. He hadn't even figured out how to unglue the earpiece from his ear.

"Hey there, Wolf."

At the sound of my voice, Marty Wolf stiffened. He turned slowly, his face a blue mask of anger.

"You ready to end this?" I offered. "One phone call, that's all it would take."

Wolf looked across the street to the theater, then back at me. "Kid, you have no idea who you're dealing with. You think I care about a couple of little pranks?" He pointed at the movie theater, the spotlights slashing back and forth like giant light sabers. "All that's for me. The Human Hit Factory is back in business. I got a hit movie about to open, and an even bigger one on the way . . . and if you think I'm going to risk all that by admitting I stole the *Big Fat Liar* idea from you, you got an even better imagination than I thought." He straightened up proudly. "See you around, Shepherd."

You know, I had to admire him. It's not everyone who could be painted blue, get their hair dyed, have their car wrecked, and be attacked by a bunch of raving Munchkins and still walk with his head held high. Yep, I had to admire that.

But it didn't mean I wasn't going to get him.

I punched a number into my cell phone and heard it click. "This is the J-Dog calling K-Bird. Repeat, J-Dog calling K-Bird."

"What the heck are you saying?" Kaylee shot back.

I frowned. Sometimes smart people took all the fun out of things. "I'm using code names now," I explained. "Wolf didn't throw in the towel. We're moving into Phase Three."

"What's Phase Three?" she asked.

"I'll tell you when we get there. Meet me at

Wolf's house. We're going to our first Hollywood soiree."

Give me credit for pulling off everything I'd pulled off so far. I mean, it's not easy to be fourteen years old and get on a plane to Los Angeles, sneak into a movie studio, and mess around with a powerful producer's life. I mean, when was the last time *you* turned somebody completely blue? Every stunt I'd pulled so far was tough, and every one of them should be preceded by one of those "Don't try this at home" warnings.

The reason I'm looking for credit is that I blew what happened next.

I didn't get into the movie.

You've got to believe I tried. I did the "I'm lost and my mom's inside" trick. I did the "Don't you know who I am?" ploy. I even tried the "Please, mister, I'm the head of the fan club" routine.

Nothing worked. Hollywood premieres are locked up as tight as Fort Knox, and to get in you need either an invitation or a good agent. I didn't have either.

So I had to settle for riding the bus into Beverly Hills and walking up to Wolf's house for the after-party. Kaylee was waiting for me.

The crowd was already arriving. Wolf had gotten there before most of them and was up in his bedroom trying to scrub off the blue dye. It wouldn't go away, but the spots where he scrubbed really hard turned into pink smudges.

Wolf grabbed a hat and pulled it low over his ears to hide his orange hair. He had changed into a casual pair of slacks and a shirt. On the way out of his bathroom, he stopped near the bed and pointed a finger at that ratty stuffed monkey. "Lock and load, Mr. Funnybones. It's go time."

Then he cruised down the stairs like he owned not only the house, but the world.

It was hard to tell if he heard any of the phrases floating above the murmurs of the crowd at his party. Most people turned away or lowered their voices as he passed by. But even so, a few choice phrases could be pulled out of the hum.

". . . worst movie I've ever seen . . ."

". . . made *Battlefield Earth* look like *American Beauty* . . ."

". . . contrived . . . painful . . . wanted to throw up . . ."

Wolf kept his head up as he glided through the crowd, ignoring the stares and looks of surprise at the sight of his blue skin. Finally he came to a stop right in front of Duncan Ross, president of the studio, who was standing with his wife.

"There he is!" Wolf said, breaking out into his widest, warmest grin. "*El presidente!* And his wife, the lovely Shaniqua!"

The woman, a beautiful lady in a flowing metallic-gray gown, frowned. "It's Shandra."

"Of course, of course!" Wolf said, not missing a beat. "Great to see you. Well, they loved the movie, don't you think?"

Duncan's face was set in harder-looking stone than usual. He paused just a moment, weighing his words, then said, "I think that sad excuse for a movie just lost the studio thirty million dollars."

Wolf swallowed hard but said, "Hey, you guys green-lit the picture."

Duncan didn't buy it. "We okayed the movie when you promised us Eddie Murphy and a chimpanzee, not Jaleel White and a chicken. You have a lot of explaining to do, Wolf. Two missed meetings, and you show up looking like a clown for your own premiere—"

Wolf held up his blue-dyed hands to hold Duncan off. "Look, look, there's a very good reason for that—"

"I don't want to hear any more of your excuses. I'm pulling the plug on *Big Fat Liar*."

"What?" Wolf's voice went up a notch. "No, you can't! You've got to give me a chance to explain."

Monty appeared at Wolf's side, having noticed the conversation from across the room. Wolf barely noticed her as he said, "Duncan, we've got history together. We're like an Oreo cookie, you and me. We're ebony and ivory. You're my brother from another mother." He punched Duncan lightly on the arm. "I'll do anything. Look, I'll even put my house up as collateral. I go another penny over budget, and this place is yours."

Duncan was unmoved. "It's over."

"Just hear me out! The truth is, I missed those meetings because . . ." He paused just a moment. "Because I had an incredible breakthrough on *Big Fat Liar,* which I was working on all day."

Duncan looked skeptical. "Breakthrough?"

"Totally!" Wolf said, gathering steam as he spoke. "I wanted to wait until we were in front of the entire industry to make my presentation."

The studio president put a hand to his chin, considering this. His eyes never left Wolf's blue-and-pink face. In a low, threatening voice, he said, "One chance, Wolf. That's all I'm giving you."

"That's all I need!" Wolf said. "Now, let me step outside to fill these lungs with a little fresh air, and I promise, you won't be sorry."

With a confident wink, Wolf whirled and headed

for the kitchen. Monty followed him. As soon as they were through the kitchen door, Monty said, "What's going on? What is this big presentation you're giving about the movie?"

Wolf clapped his hands to his head. "I have no freakin' idea! None! I was talking out of my butt cheeks!"

Monty took a step back. "You were lying to Duncan?"

"Of course I was!" the producer said impatiently. "Come on, we've got to think of something. If Duncan cancels this movie, I'm dead. My life is over. I'll be like every other poor pathetic loser out there hustling for a gig. Now, *think*!"

"I can help."

Wolf turned around and there I was, walking through the back door.

"What the . . . how did you . . . Why do you keep showing up in my life?" the producer yelled.

From the minute Wolf had made his speech to Duncan, I knew what Phase Three was going to be. Hadn't my dad said it? I had a gift for storytelling.

"Sounds like you need to come up with some big idea for *Big Fat Liar*, right?"

Wolf sputtered. "So what? Some ten-year-old is going to tell me how to save my entire movie?"

"First of all, I'm fourteen! Second of all, I created

113

that story, so I should at least be able to come up with a few good twists."

Wolf rubbed his chin. "That's true. You might actually have a point."

Monty turned to Wolf with a piercing look in her eye. "So he really did write *Big Fat Liar*?"

Wolf waved her off dismissively. "He wrote a little English paper with the same title. Big deal."

Kaylee tugged at my shoulder. "Don't do it, Jason. We've already established that he has a history of pathologically lying. How do we know he's going to keep his word?"

"We've got a witness right here," Wolf said, indicating Monty. "I swear, you get me out of this mess, I'll tell your dad you wrote *Big Fat Liar, Erin Brockovich,* and *Saving Private Ryan,* too."

I looked at Monty, but I couldn't tell what she was thinking. I looked at Kaylee, and I *knew* what she was thinking, but I also knew that I needed Wolf to agree. I looked at Wolf himself, and he was standing there with his hand over his heart, pleading with me.

Finally, I said, "Okay. Look, the story's about a guy who grows bigger every time he lies, right? So here's what we do . . ."

And then I just started talking. I don't even know where the words came from. They just seemed to pour out of me.

16
sixteen

"**Ladies and** gentlemen."

Wolf was standing halfway up his own staircase, his hands raised, drawing the attention of the crowd. He made quite a sight there, looking like he'd just flown in from a circus. Everyone fell silent.

"You're probably wondering why I'm blue and orange," he said, "and I'd like to explain to all of you . . . especially to my guest of honor, Mr. Duncan Ross, who was so patient with me today. The truth is . . . I spent the entire day enduring a torturous makeup session so that I could personally demonstrate an incredibly exciting plot twist in my new movie, *Big Fat Liar*."

He had their attention now. Every guest in the room was waiting for his next words.

"You see, *Big Fat Liar* is full of action, romance, effects, but what it lacks right now is a message. A moral, so to speak, about the human condition."

By the way, don't think Wolf memorized all this. I'd given him the lowdown in the kitchen, but he hadn't just taken it and run with it. I was still feeding him his lines. How? Because Marty Wolf still had a cell phone earpiece stuck to his ear, and I was in the kitchen, whispering into a cell phone. Funny how these things work out.

I said, "Trooper's girlfriend whips up this new potion that's supposed to make him shrink, but instead, it causes him to change colors."

When I said it, I heard the words echoed by Marty Wolf out in the living room. I went on.

"The twist is now he can't even lie about his feelings anymore. Our hero, in effect, becomes a giant mood ring."

There were murmurs from the crowd. Some of them seemed to like where this was going.

"When he's sad, he turns blue. And when he's angry"—outside on the stairs, Wolf plucked off his hat—"his hair turns flaming orange."

I stopped talking, but Wolf was going on. He said, "And when he finally realizes the ultimate truth, that he's in love with Penny, the softest shade of pink finds its way across his face."

He was taking my story and running with it. Again.

"Wolf!" I said into the phone. "You're not listening to me!"

On the stairs, Wolf grabbed hold of the earpiece and ripped. "Ahh!" he said, crying out in pain as the glue finally came unglued. He winced and said to his guests, "I . . . I'm sorry. It's too emotional. Those emotions are painful, and parts of this movie will be painful. In fact, parts of this movie have already been painful. But it gets you right here. For who among us hasn't told a little white lie?"

More murmurs, along with a few nods.

"I admit, even I've been guilty of stretching the truth from time to time. Am I proud of the one or two fibs I've told in my life? No, gang, I'm not. Which is exactly why I had to make this movie. Because our picture looks the audience in the eye and says, 'Enough is enough; lying does not cut it in this town! This cannot go on!' "

The crowd cheered, and Marty Wolf smiled.

"Anyone can make a movie with big effects, loud explosions . . . but to make a film that takes a stance, that says that the truth and the truth alone shall set you free . . . that's the real gift. That's the kind of movie a young man named Duncan Ross came to Hollywood to make. And I'm going to try my best to make him proud!"

The crowd erupted in applause. Wolf, nodding and holding his arms out in triumph, descended to walk amid the sea of admirers. He cruised among them until he washed up against the stony frame of Duncan Ross.

"Very impressive," the studio chief said. "I like where you're going with this."

"Thank you, sir," Wolf said. "Does that mean you'll approve my budget?"

Duncan nodded. "You can start shooting tomorrow. If the first day goes well, you're pay-or-play the rest of the way. You've got your two million dollars."

"Great—"

"But if anything, and I mean anything, goes wrong tomorrow, your movie, your deal at the studio, your career will be over. No more second chances. Do you hear me?"

"Dunco, I won't let you down!"

Dunco frowned deeply. "Oh, and, Wolf, I think I will take you up on your offer. You screw up, and this house becomes studio property."

A moment after that, Wolf swooped into the kitchen, his eyes flashing like the sun in the middle of his blue face. "They loved it! Duncan ate it up!

That stuff about Trooper not being able to hide his feelings was brilliant!"

"Thanks," I said. "I didn't know where you were going with that pink thing, though."

"Hey, I was just running with your idea. I gotta tell you, Shepherd, under different circumstances, we could've made a pretty good team. We're not so different, me and you."

I wasn't sure I liked the sound of that. Marty Wolf was . . . well, he was a liar.

"Are you ready to make the phone call now?"

Wolf nodded. "Let's do it."

I handed him a piece of paper with my dad's number. Wolf opened his cell phone and started to dial. I caught a look from Kaylee, a look that had *Congratulations* written all over it.

Wolf started to speak. "Hi, this is Marty Wolf. I'm standing here in my kitchen with Jason Shepherd. . . . Yup, that's the truth. I'm staring at him as we speak." There was a pause as he listened. "Okay, I'll see you in a minute. And you better bring backup."

My stomach turned. That wasn't the conversation I'd imagined. "What are you doing? I thought you were on the phone with my dad."

Wolf grinned. "Oh, I'm on the phone, but it ain't with your old man."

Three men swarmed into the room from differ-ent entrances. One of them, obviously the leader, was a square-jawed guy with pockmarks all over his face and a look that dared anyone to give him trouble.

"You're a sneaky son-of-a-gun, Shepherd," the tough guy said.

"Who are you?" I asked.

"Rocco Malone, head of security for Wolf Pictures."

Wolf slapped me on the shoulder. "Thanks for the help, kid. Saving my butt twice in one year . . . who woulda thunk it!"

I was stunned. Totally speechless. Marty Wolf had just lied to my face. A gigantic lie, in front of every-one! I couldn't believe it.

Kaylee could, and she was furious. "You can't do this!" she screamed at him. "We have a witness!"

Wolf yawned. "First lesson in Hollywood. Always get it in writing. Now get this trash out of my house."

Very big, very strong hands grabbed me by the shoulders and half-dragged, half-carried me out the back door. I had the sinking feeling that that was the last I'd ever see of Marty Wolf.

Wolf stood there with a look of pure satisfaction on his face. "I love it when a plan comes together," he said.

"How could you do that?" Monty yelled suddenly.

Wolf looked at her in surprise. "We'll discuss this later, Monty," he said.

"No, we'll discuss it now," she retorted.

They could hear party guests drifting toward them. Someone was just outside the kitchen door. "Not here," Wolf said, simmering. "Upstairs."

They marched up to Wolf's bedroom, far from the party. The minute they were inside, Wolf slammed the door closed and put a finger in Monty's face.

"Who do you think you're talking to? You're nothing; you're an executive administrative associate assistant. Don't you ever forget that!"

For a brief second, Monty looked like she would back down again. But then she shifted herself, squared her shoulders, and said, "Yeah, and I'm also the person who's written your last three movies. And for what? Whatever happened to the credit you promised me? Where's that, Marty?" Before he could answer, she went on. "It's bad enough you'd do that to me, but to steal from a fourteen-year-old kid. Do you have any morals at all?"

Wolf shrugged and replied, "Uh, not really, no. I try to leave stuff like that to the losers who aren't about to make an eighty-million-dollar movie."

Monty wrinkled her nose. Suddenly, after such a

long time, his presence disgusted her. "So that's it. You'll do whatever it takes to get ahead? No matter how many people you hurt along the way?"

He nodded. "Basically, yeah. That pretty much sums it up."

Wolf walked over to his bed and picked up the ragged stuffed monkey that lay there. "You see Mr. Funnybones over here? I love that monkey more than anything in the world. And do you know why?"

"I have my theories."

"It's the only thing left from my miserable childhood back in Paramus, New Jersey. I look at his little monkey face every morning and think, *No matter what it takes, I'm never going back there.* This isn't just a stuffed animal, Monty. This is my inspiration."

"That's touching," she said sarcastically.

He laughed. "I know. I'm actually trying to turn it into a movie-of-the-week. What do you think?"

"I think you're one of the most pathetic human beings I've ever met."

"Blah, blah," he mocked. "I guess I'll just deal with that in the next life. Now, I want you to go back to the office and write up all that emotional crap I pitched Duncan tonight."

Monty sneered. "Why don't you go do it yourself? You're the Human Hit Factory, aren't you?"

Wolf's expression turned hard and brittle. He

took a step toward her. "Hey, we have an arrangement, sunshine. The education you're getting from me is better than four years of film school."

"I've already been to film school," Monty replied. "The only thing I've gotten from you is a master class in the art of the sleazeball."

He met her gaze evenly. If nothing else had worked on him, Monty's preaching wasn't going to touch him at all. "That's worth something," he said. "Now, shoo. Get out of my face. If you want to keep your job, you'll have those new pages in my hand by the time we start shooting tomorrow."

17
seventeen

Technically, I guess it was kidnapping. I mean, Rocco wasn't a police officer, so he didn't have a right to take us anywhere. But I wasn't about to call the cops and then have to admit that I'd taken Wolf's iPAQ and snuck into his house. That wasn't exactly a solution to my problem.

So I just sat back and fumed while Rocco escorted us back to the studio and walked us into Wolf's office. I plopped myself down in a chair. Kaylee took the seat next to me. Rocco sat on the desk, staring down at us.

"I've got you trespassing on private property, stalking, stealing, conspiring to discolor a man's face and hair. We're talking at least five years in juvenile hall."

All the blood drained from Kaylee's face. "I can't go to jail. I'm a straight-A student, president of the Sigmund Freud Club, and I'm supposed to edit the middle-school yearbook!"

"You should have thought of that before you and your friend here tried to ruin an innocent man's life."

"Innocent!" I blurted. "Marty Wolf is the biggest liar in the world!"

Rocco smirked. "He's a liar? Kid, you've been lying since the minute you got here. What'd you even tell your parents, huh? Do they know you're even out here?"

I had no response to that.

"Yeah, I thought so," the security man said. "So you tell me who the real liar is." He stood up. "Look, here's how it is. Either you leave town right now, or Wolf presses charges and you both get thrown in the slammer. I'll give you a couple of minutes to think about it. I'll be outside."

I couldn't have felt any worse if Rocco had picked up a chair and hit me with it. I was beaten down. Wolf was better at this than I was. He was a bigger liar and a better sneak. The truth was, I'd never met anyone willing to go farther and get in deeper than I was. But Wolf had shown me that I was an amateur.

Realizing that I wasn't even in that league suddenly made me dislike the whole idea of lying. Before I'd met Wolf, I'd prided myself on my lies because I was the best, and it was fun being the best at something, anything—like Kaylee was the best student and Bret Callaway was the best athlete. I wasn't even the best liar.

"I . . . I'm sorry, Kay," I said. "I didn't mean to get you into this mess."

Kaylee shook my arm gently. "Come on, I came for the adventure." She stopped. "No, that's not true. I came because you're my best friend and I didn't want to let that dirtbag get away with stealing from you."

"Thanks," I said, and I meant it. Friends like Kaylee don't come along every day. "But it's over. He won. We're going home."

To my surprise, Kaylee shook her head. "We can't give up. You're Jason Shepherd! You must have a Phase Four up your sleeve."

Not really, I thought. I didn't have the energy. Nothing seemed possible. It was like I'd treated the reality of the situation like any other set of facts—I just ignored them or bent them out of shape to suit my needs. Talk about lies. The whole idea of coming to California had been one big lie—a lie I'd told myself.

That sounded like something my dad would say, and as I thought those words, I thought of him. He still loved me, I knew that much. But I also knew that he thought of me as a liar. I'd been trying for the past two days to fix that. Suddenly I realized that I'd never needed to fly across the country to solve that problem.

"Yeah," I said, finally responding to Kaylee. "Yeah, I think I do have a plan." I picked up the phone on Wolf's desk and started punching buttons.

"Hi, Dad?" I said when the phone was answered. "Yeah, it's me, Jason. I wanted to tell you. I, uh, I haven't been totally honest about what I've been up to the last couple of days. And I . . . I think it's time to tell you the truth."

Monty was in her office, typing away at "Wolf's" script, when Rocco stuck his square-jawed face into the room. "Wolf called. He's got a job for you."

Monty didn't look up from her typing. "I know. I'm doing it."

Rocco shook his head. "No, you gotta baby-sit these kids until the morning when Shepherd's parents get here."

Monty stopped typing. "What am I supposed to do with them?"

Rocco shrugged. "I don't know, you're a smart girl. You'll figure something out. Whatever you do, don't let Shepherd out of your sight."

A few minutes later Monty was escorting us out of the building and down the street to the warehouse. We had asked her if we could get our stuff together and she'd agreed, but of course she wouldn't let us go alone.

"Okay, guys," she said as we entered the big warehouse. "Pack up your stuff and we'll go wait in Marty's office."

Kaylee looked like she was hardly listening to Monty, but she did start cramming her clothes into her backpack. Then Kaylee started to talk, punctuating her words by stuffing more things into the bag. "You know what the worst part of this whole thing is? Wolf is just going to keep getting away with it. He treats all these people like dirt, and no one has the guts to stand up to him."

I shrugged. "Forget it, Kaylee."

"I can't forget it!" she said. "It makes me sick that your parents are never going to know you wrote that story."

"What are we supposed to do? We tried everything. It would take an army to get Wolf to admit the truth."

"Yeah, and everyone's too scared of losing their jobs to do anything about it. What are they all so afraid of? He's just some guy who tries to hide how insecure he is by being mean to everyone around him. Why can't anyone see that? This town is so full of wimps."

"That's it!" The words exploded out of Monty like steam that had been bottled up too long.

"What?" I asked, looking at her.

"You're right, Kaylee," the studio assistant said. "I've been pushed around by Marty for too long. I'm sorry I didn't do anything sooner, you guys."

Kaylee frowned. "It's nice that your deep-seated guilt is starting to surface, but it's a little too late, Monty."

Monty started to pace. I could see the wheels turning in her head, and I could see instantly how smart she was. She thought fast and she thought things through—you could see it in her eyes.

"Maybe not," she said, coming to a halt. "You said it'd take an army to bring Wolf down, right?"

"Yeah . . ."

"Well, I think I know where we could find our troops. Marty's entire career is on the line tomorrow. You guys up for one last fight?"

Kaylee looked at me. *It's your call,* she seemed to say.

I thought about it too. I'd already given it my best shot and Wolf had outplayed me. There was a part of me that wanted to admit I was just a kid, go home, and finish summer school. The part that had wanted to get back at Marty Wolf was pretty much gone. But there was this other, little part that wouldn't let go. It was the part that knew I'd told the truth and liked it. The part that didn't want to let go of that feeling.

"Jase?" Kaylee asked.

I nodded. "It's payback time."

18
eighteen

Marty Wolf must have awakened the next morning feeling like a million bucks. Everyone in town was saying that his chicken movie was a turkey, but he had a new movie going, with a bigger budget, and that was all that mattered. Hollywood had a short memory. It wasn't what you did yesterday, it was what you were doing today, and today Marty Wolf was starting production on the biggest movie of his career.

"It's showtime, Mr. Funnybones," he said to his stuffed monkey.

Wolf had only the slightest hint of orange left in his hair and in the right light, his skin was still a very pale baby blue.

He walked out of his house to find a stretch limo waiting for him. "You from the studio?" he said.

The limo driver, who looked vaguely familiar to him, nodded. "Yes, sir."

"Do I know you?"

The limo driver tipped his cap. "Frank Miller, sir. I was your driver until you fired me last year."

Wolf snorted. "Oh yeah. Still driving, huh? Boy, the acting career must really be taking off. Let's get moving, Brando, I don't want to be late."

He jumped in and dialed his cell phone as the limo started to roll. "Monty, it's me. I'm headed to the set. You get those pages done?"

He heard Monty speak in her usual efficient voice. "I was up all night. Everything's ready."

"Good girl. You keep this up and I may just give you an associate producer credit."

He snapped his phone shut. At the same time, the limo began to slow down, and then it pulled over to the side and stopped.

"Hey, pedal to the metal, retardo!" Wolf shouted. "I've got a movie to shoot!"

Instead, Frank got out of the car and walked to the front. He popped the hood and looked inside. Smoke billowed up from the engine.

"What's happening here?" Wolf demanded.

Frank grimaced. "We've got a situation. The, uh,

the carbide lateral valve is experiencing some serious defibrillation. Very hazardous."

Frank. A man after my own heart.

"What are you saying?" Wolf howled.

Frank made it simple. "The engine's fried. I need to call for a replacement car."

"Are you kidding?" Wolf barked. "My movie starts shooting in an hour. I don't have time for a replacement car!"

"Please!" Frank said. His eyes teared up and his hands started to tremble. "Please, don't yell at me! It's not my fault." He staggered over to Wolf, tears now streaming down his face. "It's not my fault."

Wolf leaned away from the window. "Get away from me. Stop blubbering."

"I tried so hard to do things right. I didn't want this to happen. I just wanted things to go right. It's not my fault!"

Frank was falling apart, and all Wolf could do was look for an escape route. Suddenly a candy-apple-red Ferrari rolled up beside the limo. Behind the wheel was none other than Jaleel White.

"Everything all right here?" he called out.

"I messed up!" Frank blubbered. "Real bad."

"Jaleel!" Wolf yelled in utter relief. "This is incredible. You've got to help me out here, buddy."

"Oh, yeah?"

Wolf scrambled out the other side of the limo and ran around to the Ferrari. "Look, I know we didn't quite click on the set, but that was in the heat of battle, baby. You get me to the studio in time for my first shot, I may even have a nice juicy part for you in *Big Fat Liar*."

Jaleel stared at Wolf skeptically for a moment. He seemed to be weighing his dislike for Wolf against his need to keep his career afloat. Finally he nodded. "Get in."

"Yes!" Wolf hopped into the front seat of the sports car and they took off down the road.

As Wolf drove away, Frank suddenly straightened up and wiped the tears from his eyes. *Not bad*, he thought. *Not bad at all.* He might just be ready for another audition.

We had turned the warehouse studio into a war room. Maps and blueprints were piled all around me. Right on schedule, I got a call from Frank. "J-Dog, this is the F-Man. The baton's been passed."

"Right, nice work," I acknowledged as I turned to Kaylee, who was sticking close to a map on the bulletin board. I repeated Frank's message.

"Got it," Kaylee said, tracking Wolf's progress.

I grinned. The plan was coming together.

· · ·

Jaleel White's Ferrari tore through the streets of Los Angeles at blinding speed as the young actor blasted his stereo.

In the passenger seat, Marty Wolf pressed himself back into the leather cushions and tightened his safety belt. "Nice car," he said nervously over the sound of rushing wind.

Jaleel nodded. "TV money, baby. I didn't wear those glasses and suspenders for free, dog!"

"That's a relief," the producer said. "You, uh . . . you know where you're going, uh, dog?"

"Shortcut," Jaleel explained. "Just sit back and relax, Wolfman. You're in Jaleel's hands now."

He hit the accelerator and the Ferrari's engine roared. Wolf closed his eyes in a panic. In what seemed like moments, the car was out of the city. Wolf blinked. They were driving into the desert east of Los Angeles.

"Hey, stop the car!" Wolf shouted. He craned his neck. He could see the smoggy outline of the city receding behind them. "Where are you taking me?"

"I told you, I know a shortcut!" Jaleel shouted over the wind and the engine.

"Through the freakin' desert? Slow down, you maniac! I'm getting out!"

"Your call, baby."

Jaleel slowed down but didn't stop. Wolf growled and opened the door, jumping out and tumbling along the dusty road. Jaleel waved without looking back and sped away. As he did, he thumbed his car phone and said, "Yo, this is Jaleel at the wheel. The condor has fled the coop."

Standing by the side of the road in the desert just outside Los Angeles, Marty Wolf did exactly what he always did when he was in trouble. He called Monty.

"The middle of the desert?" she said in surprise. Her acting job was almost as good as Frank's. "Marty, Duncan's supposed to be here any minute. He'll shut us down if you're not here."

"You've got to get me out of here!" Wolf shouted from the wilderness. "I don't care how, Monty. Just do it!"

If Wolf had been thinking about it—or if Wolf ever thought about anything—he might have been amazed by how quickly Monty had solved his problem. But he didn't think. He was just happy when he head the *whup-whup-whup* of a helicopter and watched the white-and-blue machine approach fast and then land a dozen yards from him.

The pilot jumped out, and Wolf recognized the

stunt coordinator Vince. Vince ducked below the spinning rotors and ran over to Wolf. "Hey, Monty said you needed help, so I grabbed the chopper from the shoot. You're in good hands, Mr. Wolf. I flew more than forty-nine combat missions in Vietnam."

"Save me the sob story, Methuselah!" Wolf snapped. "I already sat through *Platoon*. Just get me to the set!"

They both crouched low again and scurried over to the chopper. Climbing in, Vince put the headset over his ears and whispered, "This is Father Time. We are headed your way."

Flying is a lot faster than driving any day of the week, but flying over Los Angeles compared to driving through that overcrowded city was like heaven. Wolf actually felt happy for a minute, zooming half a mile above the lines of jammed traffic. As the helicopter made its approach to Universal Studios, he laughed.

But the laughter died in his throat as an alarm on the helicopter's control panel suddenly blared.

"Oh, boy," Vince said worriedly.

"What's that?" Wolf said in a panic. "What's happening?"

Vince set his jaw. "One of our blades is jammed. Come on, we have to do a forced evac!"

"A what?"

Vince tugged at his safety harness, then ran to the back of the chopper. "We've got to jump. This bird is going down!"

Wolf shrieked. "Jump! No way!"

The alarms began to blare even louder. Vince pointed to his chest, and Wolf noticed for the first time that the stuntman was wearing a thick harness and backpack. "I'm wearing a parachute," Vince said. "I think it might hold us both."

"What if you're wrong?" Wolf asked.

"Then you'll be the first to know. Come on!"

Panicked, Wolf grabbed hold of Vince. The stuntman jumped, and a second later they were cartwheeling in space, plummeting through the air.

19

nineteen

As Wolf and Vince fell, someone slipped out of a hiding place in the back of the chopper. The man calmly walked up to the pilot's seat and pressed a button. The alarms stopped. The man then sat down and steadied the chopper's flight. Then he reached for a microphone. "Chopper one to control. Father Time and the Wolf have left the building."

"I don't want to die!" Wolf screamed.

They were still in freefall. Beneath them, the ground seemed to be spinning and rushing up to meet them.

Vince laughed like he was having the time of his life. "You can't do *this* on a computer, eh, Wolf?"

Suddenly Vince jerked at something on his harness, and for a split second Wolf thought they were totally out of control. Then something big and multicolored billowed up around them, and in a quick jerking motion like a car coming to a sudden halt, they stopped falling. Wolf blinked. They were drifting now, wafting gently down toward an open field only a few hundred yards from the entrance to the studio.

Wolf and Vince hit the ground in a mass of tangled arms and legs and parachute cords. Grunting and gasping, Wolf kicked himself free and, without so much as a thank-you, got to his feet and started toward the studio entrance. When he made it to the guardhouse, he saw Leo the chubby guard staring back at him.

"Do you have a walk-on pass?" Leo asked.

Wolf's jaw nearly dropped. "Excuse me?"

"If you want to enter the studio on foot, you need a walk-on pass. Simple as that."

"Let me in, Leo!" Wolf snapped. "I've got to get to the set!"

Leo shook his head. "Not without ID. Do you have a driver's license?"

Wolf snarled. But he jerked his wallet out of his pocket and held up his license. Leo squinted, moving as slowly as he possibly could. "Let me get a closer look." He stepped out of the guardhouse and waddled slowly over to Wolf. He lifted the driver's license out of Wolf's hand and held it up, turning it over like it was a fake twenty-dollar bill. Finally he said, "Hmm. All right. You can go. And remember, bring a walk-on pass next time you hoof it to work."

Wolf snarled again, his voice hardly human. Dusty and sweaty, he jogged onto the lot and toward the *Big Fat Liar* set.

This was the moment I'd been waiting for. I was sitting on the steps of a saloon on the Western movie set. As Wolf jogged past me, I stood up and waved. "Hey, Wolf," I said casually.

"How are you, Jason?" Wolf said, moving on. Then he stopped. Frozen. Totally shocked. I waited, enjoying every minute. Slowly, Wolf turned around. He was nearly choking on his words.

"Why . . . are you . . . still here?"

I just shrugged. I had all the time in the world. "Heard you had a tough ride to work this morning. See you later. Let's go, Mr. Funnybones." I turned to walk away.

"What did you just say?" Wolf yelled.

I turned back and pulled something out of my backpack. An old, ratty monkey, the very same one that Wolf kept in his bedroom. "Oh, I was just talking to Mr. Funnybones."

Wolf's voice went cold. He squared off against me like a Western gunfighter and said in the most serious voice, "Give me back my monkey."

I smiled. "Come and get it."

Wolf charged at me. I turned and ran. I wasn't sure I could outrun him, but I wasn't really going to try. As I started to run, a golf cart tooled around a corner and pulled up next to me with Kaylee behind the wheel. "Hop on!" she said. I did, and we were off to the races.

The golf cart didn't go very fast, but it went fast enough to outrun Marty Wolf, though he wasn't about to be left behind. Another golf cart came around the corner and Wolf blindsided the poor assistant who was driving it. He climbed aboard and started after us. I didn't mind—I wanted him to follow us.

The chase led through different sets, from Chinatown to the streets of New York. On the fake New York set, stagehands were spreading snow, which was weird in the middle of summer in California. Kaylee screamed and swerved to avoid a stagehand, and the cart plowed into a bunch of Christmas trees.

"You okay?" I asked.

Kaylee blew pine needles out of her mouth and nodded. We jumped out of the cart and ran up the steps of a fake building. Behind us, Wolf jumped out of his cart and ran after us.

The minute we went through the door, we were on a totally different set—an old-fashioned set with cobblestone Mexican streets. We started running again, and we could hear Wolf behind us. He was faster than he looked, and he was gaining. As he got near, Kaylee and I both dove into a nearby alley. At the same moment, Lester Golub, computer-stunt programmer, stepped into view, holding an impressive-looking remote control. He grinned at Wolf. "Who's the Geek-Boy now, you spaz!"

He pressed a button.

Wolf heard the rumble, but he didn't move. Maybe he was too surprised to see Lester. Maybe it was just occuring to him that there was a real plot at work. Whatever the reason, he didn't get out of the way as Lester's trick released an enormous wall of water that poured onto the street. With a strangled cry, Marty Wolf was swept away by the flood.

The flood might have finished anyone else off, but not for nothing did Wolf swim every morning. He rode the flood out until he could swim to the side of the street, then pulled himself to his feet, sputtering and shivering.

Kaylee and I were waiting for him at the far end of the Mexican set. He roared and charged at us, wet, bruised, filthy, and with eyes full of rage. As he got close, we slipped between buildings and onto yet another set. As we did, Kaylee turned and hid behind a wall, whispering into her cell phone. I stayed in sight long enough for Wolf to spot me, then ran into a building and up a set of wooden stairs. I heard the *clomp-clomp* of Wolf's feet behind me, getting closer. As I reached the top of the building, a flock of fat pigeons scattered. But before I could go any farther, I felt a viselike grip around my ankle. Wolf had finally caught up to me. I tried to kick free, but stumbled, and as I did, Mr. Funnybones went flying.

For a frozen moment, Wolf and I watched the monkey fly. Then we both jumped for it, stretching out through the air like martial arts masters in an action flick. We caught the monkey at the same time and hit the ground, each of us holding the stuffed animal by one leg.

"Let go of the monkey!" Wolf yelled.

"Call my dad!"

"Never!"

Gathering his strength, Wolf wrenched the stuffed animal out of my hands. Then he stood up, towering over me.

"That's it, kid! It's over! You lose and I win!"

I looked up at him. "I don't think so, Wolf."

He laughed. "Oh, you don't think so? Come on,

Jason, you're smarter than that. You write a story, I steal it. You end up in summer school, while I'm about to start shooting the greatest movie of my life. Do the math, kid. You tell me which one of us ends up on top."

"So you admit you stole my paper?" I asked.

"It's ancient history, kid! Yes, I stole your paper, I stole your paper and turned it into *Big Fat Liar*. You know who's listening? No one! And they never will. So for the last time, give it up—because I will never, ever admit the truth."

I remembered something he'd said to me earlier. "Because the truth's overrated, right?"

"That's right!" Wolf snapped.

"And cut!"

The voice came from a bullhorn somewhere. Wolf whipped his head around, bewildered. Suddenly, from a water tower on the rooftop, a panel slid back, revealing a cameraman with his camera. On the next rooftop over, another cameraman stood up, and then another across the street, and another. Everywhere Wolf turned, there was another camera.

A crane hummed, and Dustin the director appeared, being lifted from the ground. He grinned at Wolf and said in his thick accent, "I told you, Wolf. Only way to shoot scene is from multiple camera angle!"

Wolf ran to the edge of the roof and looked down. On the street below, he saw a crowd of people—in fact, a crowd made up of every single person he *wouldn't* want to be there. There were members of the press led by Jocelyn the PR lady. Monty. Frank. Leo. Vince. And others.

And there was Duncan Ross. He'd come to watch the beginning of the shoot, of course, but when Wolf hadn't shown up on time, he'd tried to leave. Monty had asked him to stay, promising that everything would be cleared up in a few minutes.

Now Duncan stepped forward and called up to the rooftop, "Wolf! You stole the idea for this movie from a thirteen-year-old boy?"

The color drained from Wolf's face. "Well, uh, actually he's fourteen." That seemed to be all he could think of to say.

"This is the end of the line, Wolf. It's over."

Shocked, Wolf staggered back from the edge of the building. He turned to find me still there, smiling at him. I guess I just couldn't resist a parting shot. "Wolf, I just want to thank you. You taught me a valuable lesson. The truth . . . it's not overrated."

Wolf seethed. His face turned red, then black with rage. "You," he sputtered. "You. I'll kill you!"

He charged forward.

This part, I hadn't planned. I backed up, terrified

out of my wits, until I felt my feet bump against the edge of the building. Wolf was still coming toward me. With nowhere else to go, I leaned back. . . .

And suddenly I was falling through midair. I had the brief, weird sensation that I was flying—but I was only flying downward, and I was flying pretty fast—and I thought maybe it really was over for good.

And then I hit something huge and soft and forgiving, and I was okay. The next thing I knew, lots of hands were grabbing me and helping me up. When my feet were on the ground, I realized I'd fallen into the air bag the stunt team had assembled for the movie.

It took me a moment to realize that the hands that had grabbed me belonged to my father and mother. Frank the limo driver had gone to pick them up, as planned. I looked at my dad, and his eyes were as huge and soft and forgiving as an air bag.

"You did all this just to prove you weren't lying?" he asked me.

"You told me I had to earn your trust, Dad," I reminded him.

He wrapped his arms around me, the way I always remembered. "You've earned it, buddy. You've earned it."

"Hey, what about me!" Wolf yelled from above. "We've still got a movie to shoot!"

No one listened.

"Come on, people, let's make some magic!"

"Do you hear something?" asked Leo the guard.

"I'm ready to roll!" Wolf yelled, his voice growing thinner and more distant, until he could not be heard at all.

"Noise," said Frank the limo driver.

"You want to get something to eat?" offered Vince the stuntman.

Leo patted his ample stomach. "Sounds good to me."

Frank nodded. "I'll drive."

epilogue

On the movie screen, Kenny Trooper drank the vial of liquid, and suddenly he was shrinking to normal size as sirens wailed in the background. Trooper ignored them as he took his girlfriend, Penny, into his arms. "You were right, Penny. The truth . . . it's not overrated."

The picture faded to black, and as the audience cheered, the credits began to roll.

DIRECTED BY DUSTIN WONG

PRODUCED AND WRITTEN BY MONTY MORELAND

FROM AN ORIGINAL STORY BY JASON SHEPHERD

The lights went up and we stood. I fidgeted with my black tie and tuxedo jacket, which were almost as uncomfortable as summer school. But I guess that's what you wear to a movie premiere.

My parents were there, and so was Kaylee, and so were all the people who had helped.

I leaned over to Monty and said, "The new ending really works."

Monty nodded. "Thanks for the suggestion."

My dad wrapped me up in another bear hug. "I'm proud of you, son."

"You're wonderful, sweetie," said my mom.

But suddenly the Kodak moment was ruined by crowds of press people, flashing cameras and shouting. "Wonderful film, Monty!" "Nice work, Jason!" "When's the sequel?" "Is it in the works?" "How long are you going to make us wait?"

I laughed. "It's already in the works!"

"Really?" someone asked.

"Of course!" I replied. "Would I lie to you?"